Once upon a time, I might have ignored the edge in his tone. I might have written it off as nothing I'd have to worry about, as unimportant. Yes, once upon a time, I was a naïve and awfully stupid witch. That witch, though, was laid to rest weeks ago after she was murdered with broken promises and age old lies of love and trust. Her flesh was ripped from her bones, and she was left to take her last breath under a blanket of stars that he—that vile, disgusting creature—had sworn to snatch for her. The witch that stands across from Lord Mammon is someone else, something else. She's a girl, who had listened to the sound of falling stars, watched them crash in the dark and when her world was shattered and she lay in ruins, she scraped up every piece of her that had fallen to the floor, catharized her bleeding heart and rose from the ashes like a roaring wildfire, meant to burn anyone and anything in her vicinity to the ground. That witch is no longer naïve and stupid for she has become the reaper, knocking on hell's door. And as such I smell death long before it arrives.

# Hellfire & Pride

by

Nadine Nightingale

**Hellfire & Pride**

Cover Art by *Diana Carlile*

The Wild Rose Press, Inc.
PO Box 708
Adams Basin, NY 14410-0708
Visit us at www.thewildrosepress.com

Publishing History
First Edition, 2022
Trade Paperback ISBN 978-1-5092-4212-2
Digital ISBN 978-1-5092-4211-5

Published in the United States of America

## Dedication

To the girl
Who wonders if she's brave enough
Who questions if she's strong enough
To follow her desire
To carve her own path
To be her own light
You are the fire
And no one's love is ever going to burn brighter
than the one you have for yourself.

"She is both,
hellfire and holy water.
And the flavor you taste
depends on how you
treat her."

—Sneha Pal—

"He sees everything that is high;
he is the king over all the sons of pride."

—Job 41:34—

# Chapter 1

*Melissani*

The butler—a tall gray-haired man, conservatively dressed in a black waistcoat, gray striped trousers, a white shirt, and a matching gray tie—cordially beckons me into the dimly lit reception room. The entrance is flanked by two imposing bamboo palms seated in rustic cream pots, which appear to have been purposefully distressed and marked with minor faults and imperfections to add to their antique character. I run my hand down the length of the partially unlined bodice of my black lace mermaid dress, smoothing out creases from the ferry trip to the island and follow the invitation. The sight is stunning. Artful stucco has been incorporated in the round ceiling, which looms over a yellow, blue, and apricot striped, tufted walnut sofa and a set of fitting armchairs, placed on a reddish-brown Persian rug that probably cost more than the furnishings of my entire apartment.

"Take a seat, *mademoiselle*," the man says, his French accent thick. "I shall send someone to take you to the ballroom."

I lift the hem of my dress a bit higher and move gracefully over the Persian rug, careful not to break my neck in these heels. Why women wear such death traps voluntarily will always be a mystery to me. When push comes to shove, I'll always choose sneakers. "Thank

1

you." I force an appreciative smile and take a seat on the edge of the sofa, trying to look as lady-like as possible. "I really appreciate your hospitality."

He nods. "Anything for Lord Mammon's guests."

*Lord Mammon?* Well, it must be nice to bestow a title upon yourself. I should try it some time. *Lady* Melissani does have a nice ring to it, doesn't it? Lord Mammon, though? I swallow the urge to laugh and avert my gaze. It would be rude to laugh at a man who has showed me nothing but kindness. A man who should have applied for a job at Buckingham Palace rather than Castle Boldt. At least, then he'd stand a chance to return home tonight. But what is it they say? *C'est la vie,* I guess.

"Make yourself at home, mademoiselle." The butler with the poor decision-making skills bends slightly at the waist, bowing to me as if I'm a true lady, and heads back to the grand hallway.

I stay in the reception room, ogling the exquisite space. Four large rectangular windows circle the sofa, each decorated with kiwi-colored curtains reeking of supreme tailoring and plenty of money. I'm sure half of the expenses spared for the interior of this room would feed most of New York's homeless. Then again, what did I expect? Boldt Castle, built on Heart Island in the clear waters of Saint Lawrence River, was always meant to be a landmark of fame and fortune, of decadence and grandeur. According to my research, the majestic structure was built at the turn of the century by the world-famous millionaire proprietor George C. Bolt. He set out to build a full-size Rhineland castle—its beauty was meant to rival any European castle—for his beloved wife Louise. Like any good love story this one too ended in tragedy. Louise died suddenly and the poor, heartbroken George ordered all construction stopped and abandoned the project. For 73 years, the six-story, 120 room-castle, the powerhouse, the Italian gardens, the drawbridge, Alster Tower and the tunnels were left to the mercy of mother nature, withering on Heart Island like George's heart after the death of the love of his life—a single moment in time, which had left his world shattered and ruined. A fate I could relate to so well. Anyway, the structure was restored to its full glory, preserved for the enjoyment of—

"Mademoiselle Evans?" A young blond man, dressed exactly like the older man who showed me to this room, smiles at me. "You may follow me." For the record, my last name is not Evans. I made that up, just like the reason I gave to acquire an audience with the prestigious Lord Mammon. The young man, however, doesn't need to concern himself with such trivial things. He's got far bigger problems. Problems like surviving the night. He's just not aware of it yet.

With the grace of a prima ballerina, I rise from the sofa. "It's very kind of you to take me to the lord," I say, resting my gloved hand on top of his extended arm.

A genuine smile shoots over his lips. "It is my uttermost pleasure, mademoiselle."

He would never say that if he knew who I truly was and how this night will end for the guests of his treasured lord, but when kindness is given, you don't question it. You take it.

The young man guides me down the grand hallway. Fine, white Italian marble covers the floor interlaced with small black marble squares. I drink in the antique chaise lounges and armchairs; the round, gold-plated glass-top table hosting a stunning bouquet of black and red roses; and the piano, sitting beneath a large painting of an impressive Italian garden.

"It's quite stunning, isn't it?" the young man asks.

"Very much so," I say as a slight ball of regret forms in the pit of my stomach. Beauty like this should be preserved. I, however, am not much of a preserver. My métier is destruction and tonight I will revel in my talents.

We move up the oak millwork staircase. The distant sound of glasses clinking, soft jazz-music and faint conversations wafts around us, reminding me that this is nothing like the other hideouts I have hit. This place is crawling with high-ranking ruthless creatures, ready to strike at any given second.

*Keep your head in the game, Melissani.*

I will.

I have to.

For Faith's sake.

"This way, mademoiselle," my gallant guide says, heading down a wide hallway.

The unmistakable scent of cigar-smoke billows through the air as he leads me past the billiard room. I catch a glimpse of four men in suits, nurturing their brandy-glasses, while they talk business. There's not a single woman around and I can't help but snicker at the cliché. It appears as if even creatures like them fall victim to sexism. Though, that's not surprising. In fact, I believe they are the source of all the "women are the weaker gender" bullshit. In a few minutes, though, they'll learn just how weak we really are.

After what feels like forever, we finally reach the first stop on my planned visit—the ballroom. The room is breathtaking, adorned with crowned molding, dramatic lighting, and parquet flooring. It speaks of music and dancing, joy, and entertainment. The entertainment I'm faced with upon entrance was certainly not what good old George had in mind when he built this place.

Women in long ball gowns roam around, each dress made to outstand the other, they battle for the attention of...Surprise, surprise...the men. A rather impossible task, considering the eyes of said men are glued to the center of the room, where a woman with long raven hair wearing not a shred of fabric on her body, is pleasing a fellow idiot. His moans send shivers of disgust down my spine, but the others...Well, they seem to enjoy the show, queuing behind the idiot to be next in line.

I draw my gaze away from the image that will now forever be branded in my mind stamped with the words: *All Men Are Bastards Whether Human Or Not* and zoom in on a white chair next to one of the massive rectangular windows. My pulse slams against my neck as I spot the little girl, lounging on the chair, feet dangling inches above the floor. Her strawberry-blonde hair is pulled into a ponytail, her face void of any and all makeup. She wears a white dress with matching stockings, looking like a doll in the midst of monsters.

*What in the name of the goddess are you doing here, little one?*

She can't be older than eight and she's all alone. Somewhere, someone must be looking for her. Her parents wouldn't allow her to be out and about at this time of the day on a remote island. No, no parent— well, except for mine—would be okay with this.

I briefly consider her to be an innocent victim, ask myself how the hell I can get her out of here unharmed. But then she looks up, meeting my stunned gaze with confidence and self-assuredness.

*What the—*

A wicked smile creeps upon her lips as she waves at me innocently. For the untrained eye, she appears to be a sweet and kind child. She's anything but and upon closer inspection even humans could tell something isn't quite right with her. The unholy gleam in her blue eyes, the flashes of red cutting through her pupils every time she blinks are a dead giveaway to what she truly is—a monster. Just like the rest of Lord Mammon's guests.

"Do you like what you see, Mrs. Evans?" a dark voice whispers behind me.

The jolt of power radiating from the guy slices through my marrow, reminding me once more to keep my head in the game and my guard up at all times. "I might," I reply, slowly turning to face my addressor. "Lord Mammon." I flash him my best smile. "It's a pleasure to finally meet you."

"The pleasure is all mine, Mrs. Evans." He takes my hand, placing a sloppy kiss on my gloves. Gloves I must burn afterward for the fear of contagion.

I allow myself a moment to assess him. Like any rich bastard, he rocks the finest suit, made of the most exquisite fabric. He's handsome, too. Too handsome even. His styled blond hair, the abnormal ocean blue eyes and the sculptured cheekbones appear fittingly inhuman, and I'd bet my inheritance (not that there is more than regrets to inherit, but still) that he snatched this vessel from a supermodel in the making. "I hear you have an offer to make?"

Right down to business, huh? I kind of like this guy. So much so, I will thoroughly enjoy his last moments. "I do."

He nods at the door. "Shall we talk in private?"

I link arms with him, doing my very best not to shudder at his touch. "Lead the way, Lord Mammon." For it seems only right that the lamb chooses where the lion shall attack, doesn't it?

Chapter 2

*Leviathan*

The otherwise busy Georgian-style residence is empty for the night. Whereas it is usually swarmed by individuals who think too highly of themselves. It's now a mere shell inhabited by only four souls. Two of those stand guard outside the office, while the other two (of which only one is of real importance—me) are seated around a desk. The occasional creaking of the over 300-year-old house and the irritating foot-tapping of my customer adds an odd energy to the silence. One I am, indeed, quite familiar with. It is born in the deepest darkness, fed by fear and despair, and nurtured by greed and pride, just like *moi*.

"So…" My customer straightens the items on his exotic African rosewood desk, making sure everything is square and properly spaced. He doesn't suffer from OCD. He's simply dead set on avoiding my pretty face. (What a philistine!) "I've heard that you may be able to help me."

I don't bother to look at him. He's nervous as it is. Rightfully so, I might add. For I have killed better men than this blond clown simply because their presence bored me. What can I say? I hate to be bored. Just go ask Napoleon. He can tell you all about it. Oh, wait. You cannot ask him. He's dead. What a pity. I quite liked the guy. His arrogance and confidence almost

8

equaled mine. (Though, I still believe it's not arrogance when one is the best. All that miserable humbleness only messes with one's ability to reach for the stars.) "I might be," I say after taking my sweet time, enjoying the taste of his fear. It's like chocolate fudge with whipped cream.

"The matter is urgent," he replies, keeping his gaze on the golden pen systematically placed next to a stack of files on his desk.

I cross my ankle over my knee and smile. "All matters are urgent, my friend."

He looks up and hesitantly meets my gaze. "This is different."

"How so?" I feign blissful ignorance and enjoy the way it makes my new friend squirm in his over-priced armchair.

He clears his throat, quickly averting his gaze. It's a common thing. Only a few humans can withstand the beauty and depths of my eyes. In that regard, I'm like the sun—mesmerizing and magnetic yet when looked upon blinding and destructive. "I worked hard to get where I am, have done—"

"Quite a few things that put you on our radar," I finish for him, faking being impressed when in reality I already consider calling it a night to return to my laptop, where the newest episode of a British monarchy drama eagerly awaits.

His fingernails dig into the rosewood. "Anyway, I'm...I need to make sure that I stay where I am." He sighs. "Do you understand?"

I understand perfectly well. My customer has tainted his soul to occupy this mansion, this seat...And now, he needs me to keep it. Lord in hell, humans are so…So, unimaginative and simple. Once they get a taste of power, they'll do anything to get more. Power is, therefore, undoubtedly the most contagious of all viruses, plaguing the human race. It's also the most dangerous. For it infects quickly, spreads quietly and is often asymptomatic. By the time one realizes the infection, it's almost always too late. So, power-hunger and greed are two of my favorite sins. (Though, I don't want to play favorites like some parents do. It's bad for the children and for business.) "I can make that happen," I promise him.

His eyes widen. "You can?"

"Of course," I say, assuring him, and add my most charming smile, one that has led to the heartbreak of queens and the destruction of empires. I shift closer to the edge of my velvety armchair and rest my elbows on his fancy desk. "There's nothing I can't do." I pause for dramatic effect. "For the right price."

Beads of sweat drip down his forehead, gathering on the tip of his beak-shaped nose. "And what would that price be?"

I laugh wholeheartedly. Humans never cease to amaze me. There are millions of books about my kind, millions of stories, all giving away what's required of potential customers when striking a deal with my kind. And yet here he sits, feigning ignorance. How amazing. "Don't worry about the price just yet." I lean back in the comfortable chair. (I should ask him where to find such magnificent furniture. My back would thank me for it.) "Tell me what you need me to do first."

He inhales a sharp breath. "I…I made promises I can't keep."

Of course, he can't keep them. They were blatant

lies, and he knew it. "And?"

"And now people are growing tired of me."

"They are," I say, having witnessed the uproar outside his residence myself. All that anger floating about is better than the all-you-can-eat buffet at my favorite Thai restaurant.

He picks up his golden pen, rolling it between his thumb and forefinger as if that will help him. It doesn't. It just makes him look desperate. A look he wears quite well. "I need to show them that I'm the only one who can get them through these difficult times."

"As any narcissist does," I murmur under my breath.

"What?"

"Nothing," I say, gesturing for him to continue.

"They need to understand that they're lost without my guidance." He stops fiddling with the pen and meets my gaze. "They need to see that I'm the only one who can protect them."

Oh Satan, how mundane. Men like him, men in power are often the epitome of uninspired. It's as if even the Muses grew tired of their dullness and left them to rot in their uncreative prison cells, only for me to find them and restore them to their former glory. (All right, that might be an exaggeration, because as amazing as I am—and I am the most amazing of them all—I can't make this creature glorious. Not even the big guy in the sky can.) "So, what do you need me to do? Start a war?"

He laughs as if I made the best joke ever. "A war?" When I don't join in, he sobers up and sits a little straighter. "You can do that?"

Can I do that? "I ended Cesar's reign by goading

his loyal senators into killing him." I shrug. "There's really nothing I can't do." Well, except endure this pathetic creature much longer.

Utter fear creeps into his eyes. "Y-you did what?"

I wave the question off. Mostly, because I don't feel like talking about the arrogant Roman prick. (He believed himself smarter and more cunning than *moi*. Can you believe that? As if anyone could be smarter or more cunning than me. The audacity). "Just tell me what you need me to do." I lift a warning finger. "And be very specific."

"I…" He shifts uneasily. "I…"

"You?"

"I'm not sure, if this meeting was the best idea. Maybe we should—"

"Relax," I say, snatching the photo from his desk. "We're all friends here." I run a finger over the bright face of his daughter. "Aren't we?"

## Chapter 3

*Melissani*

Lord Mammon, as he refers to himself these days, shuffles me out of the ballroom, past leering men—distracted by the long slit in my black dress, exposing my bare skin beneath it—and into the wide hallway. Paintings that belong in the Louvre plaster the biscotti-colored walls and the wooden furniture are either exact replicas of woodwork created at the turn of the century or indeed antique relics that survived the hands of time. Either way, the sight is impressive, and I cherish it, because after tonight no one else ever will.

The so-called lord guides me past closed doors toward the end of the hallway and stops at the second to last door on the right. "After you," he says, opening the door like the gentleman he'll never be.

"Thank you." I walk into a rather simplistic suite. There's a wooden bed, an armchair and a small escritoire surrounded by three large windows with flowery curtains—compared to the rest of the castle it appears almost too plain.

"Do you like it, Mrs. Evans?" Mammon asks as he shuts the door behind us.

I scan the ordinary room and shrug. "It's all right."

Mammon flashes me an innocent smile. "A little dull for my taste," he says as he takes off his jacket and starts rolling up his sleeves. "But it serves tonight's purpose."

Once upon a time, I might have ignored the edge in his tone. I might have written it off as nothing I'd have to worry about, as unimportant. Yes, once upon a time, I was a naïve and awfully stupid witch. That witch, though, was laid to rest weeks ago after she was murdered with broken promises and age old lies of love and trust. Her flesh was ripped from her bones, and she was left to take her last breath under a blanket of stars that he—that vile, disgusting creature—had sworn to snatch for her. The witch that stands across from Lord Mammon is someone else, something else. She's a girl who had listened to the sound of falling stars, watched them crash in the dark and when her world was shattered and she lay in ruins, she scraped up every piece of her that had fallen, catharized her bleeding heart and rose from the ashes like a roaring wildfire, meant to burn anyone and anything in her vicinity to the ground. That witch is no longer naïve and stupid for she has become the reaper, knocking on hell's door. And as such I smell death long before it arrives. "And what is tonight's purpose?" I ask never ceasing to smile.

Lord Mammon turns to face me. His eyes no longer blue but the color of wrath. "You tell me, my dear Melissani *Evans*." He cocks a brow. "Or would you prefer I call you by your real name, Ms. Douke?"

"You're not dumb after all," I reply calm and good naturedly.

Lord Mammon narrows his eyes. "Why are you really here, Melissani?"

"Well." I wander through the suite, take off my gloves and place them neatly on the escritoire. "You see, I'm in need of information." I face him with a crooked grin. "And I was hoping, you, the great Lord Mammon"—I make a grand gesture to emphasize how ridiculous his title sounds—"could help me attain it."

He balls his fists and eyes me like a predator, contemplating his next move. "Even if I could," he finally hisses. "I would never help the likes of you."

"The likes of me?" I laugh.

His nostrils flair. "Does that amuse you?"

"It does," I say. "For you know as well as I do there is no one like me."

He pulls his shoulders back, tilting his head. "No," he agrees. "There's no other abomination like you and I thank Satan for it."

Dear goddess, why are creatures like him always so melodramatic? "I only have one question," I say, drawing a calming breath. "Answer it to my satisfaction and I will grant you a quick death. Lie to me or do anything stupid and I will make your end hurt."

Lord Asshole throws his head back and laughs. The sound is so obnoxious I worry about my eardrums. "Little witch," he says, catching the tears in the corner of his eyes with his pinky finger. "You are indeed amusing, and I appreciate your pride." He arches a brow. "Not many would have dared to enter my castle with the plan to threaten my existence. I can therefore see why our Crown Prince was so taken with you. However"— his eyes burn like molten lava—"I do not appreciate your tone, nor do I appreciate your threats. So, why don't you say a last prayer to your puny goddess before I have the pleasure of sending you to hell." He cracks his knuckles

"Don't worry, Lord." I bite my lower lip and smile. "I've already said my last prayer." Though it was more like an oath that I took. An oath that demands retribution for every wrong he did to me. One I intend to fulfill no matter the circumstances. For I swore to be his reckoning. "Did you?" I ask in return as I welcome the tiny spark of hellfire, born in the depths of my rotten soul, snaking through my veins only to rise to a glorious flame in the center of my left palm.

He stumbles backward, well aware what the fire can do to him. "Do you honestly think you can scare me with this party trick?"

"I do." I eye the fire, rising and falling along with my chest. "Because this trick, Lord Mammon, will be the last you ever see." That said, I toss the flame at the floor in front of him. Within the blink of an eye, it claims his pants, fighting its way upward.

He screams. Screams like they all did, before they met their maker. "Stop this!"

"Oh, I'm sorry," I say. "But abominations like me don't take orders from the likes of you, my lord."

The flames bite through the fabric of his pants, quickly working their way through seven layers of skin to reach his shinbone. "Please," he begs, dropping to the floor. "Please, stop!"

"Since you asked so nicely," I say, snapping my fingers to extinguish the flames seconds before they reach his loins.

He convulses on the floor, crying like a baby. Amazing how quickly strong, feared monsters turn into whining little boys. "So." I move toward him, looking down at the mighty demon of wrath. "Would you care for a civilized conversation, or shall I burn off the rest of your disgusting flesh right away?"

He tries to drag himself backward, away from me.

It's useless. His leg is burnt, exposing bone. Divine justice is what I call it. Or maybe just an eye for an eye. Whatever suits you. "W-what do you want?"

I kneel, caressing his cheek and searing it with my bare touch to leave a scar that will forever brand him as the demon of wrath who got marked by...What did he call me again? Ah, right, an abomination. "Tell me where he is."

"I don't know," he barks.

"Wrong answer," I say, running my hand over his left eye. The heat of my touch slowly boils the blood in his eye. The crimson liquid hisses like an angry snake. A moment later, his eye pops like corn in a saucepan. Jesus, the stink...Disgusting.

He screams some more. The high-pitched tone is annoying as hell and I'm starting to wonder if the mighty demon's mother could have been a siren or perhaps a fury. His family relations really don't matter, though. His suffering does and I wish I could say it disturbs me. It doesn't. Like every good reaper, I've come to enjoy the despair of my victims greatly. However, I'm well aware that his screams will draw the attention of others and, therefore, I must rush the matter, whether I like it or not. "Where is he? Tell me."

He shakes his head, burned flash dangling off his face, the remains of his left eye sprinkled across his cheek. "He will kill me."

"I will kill you," I promise.

Mammon's good eye moves over my face. "Why are you doing this?"

"Because I can," I reply, slightly scorching his chin. "Now, tell me where your damn crown prince is!"

"He's—"

"Lord!" The door bursts open. "Lord, what—" The horde of demons stop dead in their tracks as they spot their leader on the floor, crying like a little girl. "What the fuck?" one yells, his brown eyes turning blacker than a starless night.

"Great," I murmur, slowly rising to my feet. "I was this close"—I show them with my thumb and forefinger—"to making the asshole talk. But you just had to come and fuck it up, didn't you?"

For a moment, a dozen clueless eyes stare at me. Then one of the idiots shouts, "Kill her!" And just like that my last hope of getting his location goes up in flames. Quite literally and in every sense of the word.

## Chapter 4

*Leviathan*

Terror. It starts with a grain of fear planted in one's mind—fear of the dark, fear of the unknown, or like in this case fear of the handsome devil you called and can't get rid of now. "I do have another meeting to attend to," my customer murmurs, watching me closely as I return the photo of his sweet angelic daughter to its rightful spot on his desk. "M-maybe w-we can...P-pick this up some other time?"

I lean back and laugh casually. A laugh I don't need to fake because this man...He amuses me greatly. See, when he asked for my help (begged really), he said, and I quote: "I'll do anything."

"Anything?" my assistant had asked him. "You might want to be careful with such promises, my dear. Because where I am from, we trade in promises that cannot be taken back."

"Anything," he had repeatedly assured her.

Now look at him. He's shaking. His fear inflates like a balloon, slowly transforming into pure and utter terror. I can already taste its sweetness on the tip of my tongue and it's oh so delicious. Yet not nearly as potent as it will be when I'm done with him. "I would think it quite rude to arrange a meeting with a potential new friend only to cut it short ahead of time, wouldn't you?"

He swallows so hard his Adam's apple bops. "Of

19

course, yes. No, I…"

"Yes or no?" I push, never allowing my smile to falter.

"It would be rude," he agrees, polluting the air with his fear. "The other meeting can wait."

"It can," I agree. Who wouldn't want to spend more time in my company? Only a fool. And he is no fool. Fine, he is a fool, but that's beside the point. "Now, let's talk about those plans of yours."

"Y-yes…O-okay."

Have I ever mentioned how awful the human race's communication skills are? They simply cannot master the art of words. Even the best of them—men like Shakespeare and Goethe (I adored them both for they had a gift with words, even if only on paper, and they had both entertained me greatly during countless boozy nights in the past.) could never quite express themselves the way a man should. You know, with certainty, wisdom, and confidence. Like me, basically. "Since the subject of war seems to make you a bit uncomfortable, I suggest you tell me what you had in mind when you asked for my assistance."

He draws a deep breath, pulls himself together and finally spills the beans. "I need to make good on my promises."

"Your promises?" I chuckle. Even if heaven and hell combined forces it would be next to impossible to perform a miracle that would allow him to make good on the falsehoods he fed his people. I am curious about his ideas though. "How?"

He folds his hands in an effort to hide the trembling. "I had most of my fellow heads of state convinced," he says, his face going sour, like a pint of milk left out in the sun. "But she wouldn't budge."

She is smart. So much smarter than the men running their countries in the ground. "So…" I inch closer. "Tell me, what do you want me to do about that?"

"If it weren't for that obnoxious woman," he says, giving voice to the envy rising inside of him like toxic smoke. "None of this would have happened."

"True." And not. See, what my lovely customer doesn't understand is there will always be a woman like her. A woman who follows reason instead of an inflated ego. It's always been like that. Women, although referred to as the weaker gender, have always been the stronger part of any equation. They don't allow their egos to get in the way and make informed decisions based on what's best for them and anyone around them. The boss blames evolution for it. Women are born to give life and their instincts tell them to protect it by any means necessary, even at the expense of their own safety. Men, on the other hand, are born to kill, to feed only those closest to them. Personally, I'd like to believe it's their intelligence that outranks most men. (Not mine, though. No one is smarter than I am.) Why do you think men came up with that fraudulent story of Eve being seduced by our lord and is therefore to blame for the exile from Eden? Anyway, I can see where this is headed. "So, what shall we do about her?"

"She needs to go," he barks, no longer reigned by terror but by anger and the need for more power.

"Go where?" I lean back and smile. "The Bahamas? Bali?" I cock a brow. "I told you to be very specific."

"Kill h—" The door bursts open, cutting him off

mid-sentence.

I turn, ready to make the idiot who dared to interrupt pay, when I spot one of my customer's guards, barging in like the house is on fire. I would torture him, but one look in his purple eyes changes my mind. "Sala?" I smile at my assistant. "Nice meat suit." On any other day, my assistant rocks the vessel of a beautiful slightly crazy chick, but she obviously left her meat suit behind to travel quickly. That's just one bonus of being a demon. When we need to get somewhere fast, we simply shed our skins and possess some poor bastard.

She frowns and stops dead in her tracks. "This is not the time for smart-ass comments."

"But why?" I give her an incredulous look. "You wear testosterone fueled, brainless muscle quite well, my dear."

Usually, Sala would smack me for such a comment. She loves being a woman and she also loves women per se. Today, however, her expression is a mixture of "this is bad" and "this is so bad, we might die." "We have to go."

I nod at my customer, who sits frozen in his fancy armchair, glaring at his former security guard taken over by my assistant as if she were an alien. "But I was just going to—"

Sala closes the distance between us, puts her hands on both sides of the armchair and whispers, "It's her, Lev. She burned down Castle Boldt and everyone in it."

"She did what?" I yell. "B-but why?" I stammer, suddenly lacking the communication skills I pride myself on.

Sala sighs. "She's looking for you."

"How do you know?" Maybe she just felt like lighting a bonfire and confused the castle with a stack of wood.

"Because she left one of them alive to tell the tale." Sala produces a charred piece of paper from her pocket. "Look for yourself."

I gape at the words. Words written in blood. They read: "You can run little demon, but you can't hide. Sooner or later, I will strike you down."

"Shit." I get on my feet. Well aware Sala is right. "We do have to go." And find a rock to crawl under. Am I scared? Of a witch? Hell, no! I'm just…Well, let's just call it survival instinct, shall we?

In that exact moment, my client's voice returns. He's not just boring and annoying as hell, he also has shitty timing. "But what about me? What about our deal?"

"Ah, yes, about our deal." I turn to face him. "It's not going to happen."

"Why?"

"Because you do bore me," I say with a lazy shrug. "And I hate being bored." Then I snap my finger and my new friend goes straight into cardiac arrest. Tomorrow, the news will announce a heart attack and he will get all the fame and love from his people he so longed for. Isn't that ironic?

Chapter 5

*Leviathan*
One week later.

There are few things I abhor more than low-grade, tedious business meetings. Low-grade, tedious business meetings held inside a long-abandoned manor, reeking of regrets and pitiful human existences which end in despicable but well-deserved deaths are definitely one of them. I'd love to skip this inferior shit-show. I mean, I have souls to taint, empires to destroy. Yet here I am, strolling through a musty smelling, dimly lit manor, hosting old, stained furniture, appearing as if it'll crumble to dust if I accidentally touch it.

*Fun times, huh?*

I cross the gigantic foyer, passing boarded-up windows laced with cobwebs and portraits of generations of self-righteous folks that once occupied this mansion. Heads held high, noses stuck in the sky, they look down on me as if I were the one who enslaved hundreds of women, children, and men, making them work in the cotton fields down the road, abusing and slaughtering them every chance I got. Newsflash: it wasn't me. As a matter of fact, I always steered clear of plantation owners. (I couldn't stand the scent of those filthy bastards. They reeked of chewing tobacco, sweat and blood. Disgusting.) Even in 1863, when chattel slavery ended in most places due to Union measures such as the Confiscation Act and the Emancipation Proclamation quite a few plantation owners were desperate enough to try to conjure me, I refused to answer their calls. Enslaving anyone based on their skin color and ethnicity is simply stupid and inappropriate. Where I'm from, we judge people for their souls, because vessels are temporary, one's essence, however, usually lasts forever. But sinners always tend to cast the first stone. That irony never gets old.

Reaching for the metal doorknob of the ailing oak door, I catch a glimpse of the mold, eating away at the walls and the wood flooring.

That's just gross.

And so unnecessary. I'm well aware the boss loves run-down places. They feed into the image he built for himself over the past centuries, but those were different times. If you ask me, it's about time to take our business to the twenty-first century—iPads, decent five-star hotel conference rooms, spas, and all. But I guess beggars can't be choosers, and so I turn the knob, push the squealing door open and saunter into the great hall.

Heads turn.

Conversations dissolve into faint whispers.

And dozens of gleaming eyes follow my every move.

A smug grin plastered across my face, I head straight for the make-shift bar—an antique hostess-trolley stacked with several bottles of the finest and oldest whisky mankind has to offer.

A tall, brunette, eyes the color of molten rubies, greets me with a smile that holds wicked promises of unholy pleasure. "What can I do for you, handsome?"

She purrs like a sweet kitten that's about to bite off my man-parts.

My gaze darts to her massive cleavage spilling out of her too tight top like tequila overflowing a shot glass. Those two ladies must have led armies of poor bastards straight into the first circle of hell—the one ruled by lust. "How about some good old Macallan?" I say, never taking my eyes off her eyes...Yes, I'm staring at her eyes, not her boobs. (Come on, did you expect the crown prince of hell to be a peeping Tom? How rude and judgmental of you.)

She pours me a shot of the good stuff and hands it over. "Anything else?" she asks, playing with the silver piercing sticking in her rosy tongue.

Well aware she's offered more than just another beverage or nuts to go with it, I let out a frustrated sigh. As tempting as her proposal is, I don't have time to show her why millions of women would sell their souls to share my bed. The meeting is about to start, and I want it to end as quickly as possible. Giving Miss Cleavage a taste of my awesomeness will have to wait. "I'm fine for now, sweetheart."

"I'm just a call away," she says, before I make my way to the front row table where my siblings kindly saved me a spot.

Berith casts me a sidelong glance. "You're late," she hisses as I put my drink on the table, joining her and a grumpier than usual looking Verin.

I shrug my favorite (fine, my only) sister's comment off. "I'm a busy man."

Verin runs a hand through his short, chestnut-colored hair and shakes his head. "You've been hiding this past week," he says as if I needed a reminder. Me, the biggest fish in hell, who has never spent a day in all his demonic existence hiding. "How busy could you have been?"

"Very," I say.

Berith secures a strand of her wavy silver-blonde hair behind her ear and assesses me with her pale gray eyes. "You do realize this is serious, right?"

"Of course, business always is." I take a sip of whisky. "Just because I'm a little restricted in my movements doesn't mean I've neglected the needs of my customers. That's bad for business. Also, why do you think I downloaded the Zoom App on my computer?"

Verin's eyes go wide. "You're doing business on Zoom?"

I cock a brow. "Welcome to the twenty-first century, brother." Since I'm offering my services online, I barely get time to watch that new show I got hooked on. This morning, for example, I had to deal with my client's Hollywood drama. Took me a solid three hours to convince the diva that killing off all of her competition wasn't what we agreed on when she made her deal. Come on, one weird accident could be shrugged off as a tragedy. Slaughtering half of the actresses in Hollywood? Well, that would be a bit too obvious, and the boss would go nuts. There are laws in hell even I have to abide by—making sure our existence remains a secret is the most important one.

"Busy or not…" Verin shoots me a sidelong glance. "You're fucked, Lev." My brother would have been a superb novelist. He tends to dramatize even the most trivial things.

"Don't you think you're overreacting?" It's been a

week since the incident at Castle Boldt and so far, I haven't heard of any other demon murders. Maybe she really did mistake the castle for a stack of wood.

"He's not," Berith murmurs.

"I'm not," Verin assures me. He points at Abbadon, also known as the duke of destruction or the bosses' favorite pet. The bastard's liquified blue eyes pierce mine. "He hates your guts, Lev, and judging by his smug expression he's got something up his sleeve. Why else would he have arranged this meeting?"

It pains me greatly to admit it, but my siblings might be on to something. See, Abbadon isn't exactly known for his social skills. The duke of destruction barely shows his face in public these days. He's a weirdo, who collects all things *Hello Kitty* in his spare time and tortures his clients when he's on the clock. Organizing demon gatherings just doesn't fit in his schedule and I'm fairly certain he's planning some crazy bullshit, which I won't like. Still, I couldn't care less about him and his madness. "Abbadon can go fuck himself. Might be good for him, considering no one else will." (I don't usually revert to such language, but Abbadon has always had that effect on me.)

Abbadon's eyes narrow. He heard me loud and clear, but he knows better than to challenge me. He witnessed legions of stupid idiots, suffocating on their own blood, because they were dumb enough to mess with me. Bastard or not, he's smart enough to keep his hatred in check and his envious mouth shut.

Berith shifts closer, lowering her voice to a whisper. "Have you heard what she did last night?"

"Who?" I say, pretending I have no clue about what—or should I say who—she's talking about, when in reality I'm dying to get the latest news about her mad rampage. News I must have missed, because I was too busy watching my new show instead of answering Sala's hundred calls. They went straight to voicemail, and I swear, I wanted to check my mailbox. I just got a little sidetracked with all the drama on TV and in my client's life.

Verin frowns. "You know damn well who!" My brother's anger issues get worse by the day. Soon, we'll have to find him a good therapist. Preferably before he ends up like our father.

"No clue," I reply, keeping up the charade. Hey, old habits die hard and a notorious liar like me isn't just going to change his ways.

Silence wraps around the great hall, killing hushed conversations. A few eerily quiet moments later, Abbadon rises from his chair to face the eagerly waiting and hellishly curious crowd. "Friends," he starts his lame speech. "I'm thrilled all of you could make it." His gaze shoots to me. "Especially you, Lev."

I keep my face straight and take a sip of whisky to swallow the disgust sitting on the tip of my tongue. Abbadon and I are like puppies and kittens—we just don't get along. He's old-school. I'm innovative. He also never got over the fact the boss trusts me with all the important stuff. Hey, I will be taking over his throne one day. It's only fair I get to run the show, isn't it?

"I won't keep you waiting any longer and will get right on to the reason for this get together," Abbadon says, obviously enjoying the attention of the crowd. He's always been hell's attention whore. (Why do you think he dresses in pink and uses a *Hello Kitty* phone?) Another reason he loathes me—when I walk into a room all eyes are on me. I'm mesmerizing like that.

"It's her, isn't it?" Luvart, a third hierarchy demon, blurts out, his voice tarnished with something that sounds a hell of a lot like fear. "She's completely out of control."

Abbadon nods. "You're right, old friend. She's on a killing-spree. A bloody one, I might add."

"We need to stop her," someone yells from the back.

"Kill her," another chimes in.

"Yes!" the crowd cheers, throwing their fists in the air. "Kill the damn witch!"

Berith eyes me with concern, but there's no reason for her to worry. I have had centuries to learn how to keep my wrath in check. A couple of low-level demons and their need for revenge aren't going to ruin years of yoga. Also, I meditate. Daily.

Abbadon straightens, forcing his spine into an unnaturally rigid position. "You're right. The witch is a liability, and she needs to go, so I'm here to ask our treasured prince." The bastard flashes me a stab-worthy smile. "What are you going to do about her?"

All eyes rest on me. Anticipation builds, wrapping the place in a thick blanket of questions and expectations.

I guess I should say something. Anything. But I've never been one to play by the rules, so I lean back, down my whiskey and smile.

"Leviathan," Abbadon's voice thunders through the hall. "Did you not hear my question?" He points at the crowd. "*Our* question?"

"Sorry, Ab. Your ugly face distracted me." I slam the empty glass onto the table and force a sweet smile.

"So, what was the question again?"

Abbadon frowns. "What are you going to do about the witch?"

"Ah, yes. The witch." I tap my finger against my temple. "Well, old *friend*, what do you want me to do about her?" It's not like I can snap my fingers and make her go away.

Abbadon narrows his eyes. "It's time for you to kill her, don't you think?"

"Kill her?" I laugh harshly. "We are speaking about the same witch, aren't we?" Many of my brothers have tried to off her. The lucky ones were turned to ash, their essences taken to purgatory for eternal torture. The not so lucky ones? Well, let's just say there are worse fates than death and eternal damnation.

"She hit one of our bars last night." Abbadon glares at me. "Three Legions were obliterated."

"Three legions, huh?" Well, she is a busy bee, I have to give her that. Then again, she's always been focused and once she sets her mind on something, no one can stop her. (Not even my mesmerizing self.)

Abbadon slams a hand onto the hip of the vessel he's currently rocking—a twenty-something dude with enough fast-food flab on his hips to make him the prime example as to why burgers are the real evil in this world. It also speaks of the carelessness of the human race. They get one vessel for a lifetime and instead of taking care of it, they run it down like it wasn't supposed to last. I'll never understand that. Look at me, I have worn this vessel for thousands of years and it still looks as perfect as it did on the day I snatched it, but whatever. Human fast-food addictions and their need for self-harming aren't my problems. Abbadon is and he's all set to continue his wretched speech. "You, Leviathan, are the crown prince. It is your duty to protect us."

"My duty?" I laugh so hard the echo can surely be heard in hell. "Who do you think I am? Mother Teresa? Nelson Mandela? The European Union?" Protecting anyone but myself is as foreign a concept to me as compassion, love, kindness, and loyalty. Abbadon of all demons should know that.

Hateful gazes pierce my back, while shocked whispers roar through the hall. "He doesn't care…"

"He should care…"

"He's a brat."

I don't care about their assessment of my character, and I refuse to play Abbadon's stupid game. Because the idiot is right about one thing: I *am* the crown prince of hell. I do what I want when I want. And killing her has never been on my to-do list. Fine, it has but that was before…Never mind. "She's not my problem."

"She's killing legions," Abbadon yells, the vein in his left temple pulsating fiercely. "And you refuse to interfere? Don't you care about the fate of your faithful subjects?"

"I don't," I admit, arms crossed above my chest.

Berith shakes her head. "What are you doing?" she hisses quietly.

"Securing himself a spot in the ninth circle is what he's doing." Verin grunts.

Did I mention that my siblings are a wee bit dramatic? The ninth circle is reserved for the most treacherous bastards, the ones dumb enough to betray the boss. And while I might play by my own rules, I'd never cross him. I've seen what he does to traitors and

I, as well as all of womanhood, treasure my testicles.

Abbadon runs a hand through his shaggy blond hair and smiles. "So, let me get this straight. You are hereby refusing to fulfill your duty, is that what you're saying?"

He likes to play, huh? Let's play then. "Who says that killing her is my duty?"

"I do." His deep, smooth voice chills my cold heart to the core, raising goosebumps over my skin.

Abbadon, along with every other demon in the room, drops to their knees, lowering their heads. "My king."

I should probably kneel too, but I'm not the knee-dropping follower kind. What can I say? I detest generation social-media and the boss knows it. Which is why he ignores my disrespect and strolls to the front of the room with the grace of a false god, who has deceived nations. "Rise," he orders.

Abbadon is quick to jump to his feet. "My lord." He bows again. "It's been too long."

The boss ignores him and faces me with a look that could slaughter billions. "She's out of control," he barks, his chiseled jaw hard and unforgiving. "And you know it, son."

I do, but that doesn't change a thing. "She'll come around."

"When?" the boss hisses, red flashes sparking in his heavenly blue eyes.

Hopefully, sooner rather than later. "She's just—" I cut myself off before I vomit words like hurt and disappointed—trivial human emotions the boss surely won't care about. Not when she's wreaking havoc by executing his best and most loyal warriors Jeanne-d'Arc-style.

Abbadon steps forward. "My king," he addresses the boss, gaze low. "May I speak freely?"

The boss gestures for him to speak. "Please do."

Abbadon, the treacherous snail, flashes me a grin and straightens his back. "We have suffered great losses." He shoots me a dark look. "The witch must be stopped before it's too late."

"You're right." The boss faces me. "And that is why you will end her, son."

"What?" I ball my fists, certain my hearing malfunctioned. The boss did not just order me to kill her. No, he wouldn't. Or would he?

"You heard me," he shoots back, the unchecked anger in his voice rattling the walls.

Molten lava floods my veins. A hurricane of unfamiliar emotions rushes my system. He wants me to kill her? That's... "What if I refuse?" I hear myself ask, not even considering the consequences of such a stupid question.

"If you refuse..." The boss approaches me like a lion stalking his prey and rests a hand on my shoulder. "*I* will end *you*." He pauses, searching my eyes. "Do I make myself clear?"

The boss's angelic smile sends cold shivers down my spine. My mouth is drier than the desert, but I force my tongue into action. "Yes."

"You've got three days," he announces.

"Three days?" I laugh. "And how do you propose I end her in three days?" It's not like I can call her or knock on her door to slam a knife through her heart. She'd burn the flesh off my skin before I could cross the threshold. She's resentful like that.

The boss smirks. "Why don't you use your charm, son? Isn't that what got us into this mess in the first place?"

That and the witch's obnoxious beauty along with her fearlessness and her dirty mouth, but I'm not nearly stupid enough to mention that.

"Three days," the voice of the boss echoes through the silent room even though he's long gone.

A hand lands on my shoulder. "I am so going to enjoy this," Abbadon says, grinning like the ugly bastard he is.

"A lot can happen in three days," I hiss through gritted teeth, fighting the urge to slit the throat of his ridiculous vessel to send his stupid ass back to hell.

"Is that so?" he challenges.

I shrug. "You never know which demon is next on her list, do you? Would be a shame if you burned before she does, wouldn't it?"

He's smart enough to recognize the underlying threat in my voice and eventually retreats to his table, leaving me with Berith's pitiful looks and Verin's "I told you you're fucked" expression.

Chapter 6

*Melissani*

The instant the old, weak, and susceptible Melissani perished and the new me was born, I understood fear was less of a safety trigger, installed in our brains to warn us of approaching danger, and more of an obstacle, hindering us from reaching our full potential. Fear's currency, I learned quickly, are all those useless "what if" questions endlessly plaguing our minds:

*What if I'm not brave enough?*

*What if I'm not strong enough?*

*What if I can't go through with it?*

*What if he looks at me like he did when he spun his lies of love and happiness?*

*What if I die before I can save her?*

If I were to become hell's reaper, I couldn't allow myself to be distracted by such questions. So, in order to become his reckoning, I rid myself of fear's influence and shed the emotion like a snake sheds its skin. I became that fearless thing, walking right into the mouth of the monster, ready to knock its teeth out from the inside. (Yes, it's an odd metaphor. Blame Jonah and the Whale for it.) Anyway, the point is I don't blink easily and very few places give me the creeps. Georgina's cottage—in the middle of this godforsaken, haunted forest—is one of them. Even for someone like me, it's easy to see why locals avoid this part of the woods. The urban legends surrounding this place are darker than a starless night. They're composed of lost, never-seen-again children, gingerbread houses, cannibalistic back-wood witches, and a lot of other nightmare-invoking material. Not exactly surprising when you take into account the ramshackle cottage decorated with bones and drawings of all kinds of witchy symbols. I've never been one to judge a book by its cover. In this case, however, I'm inclined to make an exception. Because every witch in the western hemisphere knows good old Georgina is every bit as rotten as the cottage she resides in.

"Calm down, Melissani," I tell myself, trying to forget the dread crawling down my spine. "She hates those bastards as much as you do." Maybe even more so. Word on the street is a demon slaughtered her daughter during her initiation rite. Apparently and understandably, the witch never got over the death of her only child and withdrew to these woods, where she's supposedly conjuring demons to feed to her cats. Okay, the whole cat-thing might be another urban legend, but Georgina and I are on the same page when it comes to those bitches and I'm hoping she'll assist me in this most urgent matter.

Hiding my shaky hands in the pockets of my biker jacket, I move up the weeping stairs leading to the porch. A single lantern burns on a wooden table next to the door, illuminating the dark night and shedding light on a bunch of bones hanging from the roof. I recognize the skull of a large cat.

*Gross.*

I'd be seriously pissed at the witch for displaying

the remains of that poor animal, but despite Georgina's reputation I know she didn't hurt that cat. Georgina is a bone-witch. She draws her powers from the remains of humans and animals alike. That doesn't mean she flies around on a broomstick looking for victims she can skin alive. No, Georgina follows the path of Gaea. Most elemental-witches like myself worship the goddess of earth and we would never hurt her creation intentionally. Neither would good old Georgina. Well, she wouldn't hurt animals. Can't say the same about humans or other witches. Georgina has slaughtered covens and continues to kill anyone who hurts the inhabitants of these woods. The reason why no one in their right mind would show up on her doorstep unannounced. What the hell am I doing here? Well, I never claimed to be sane, did I?

I'm still staring at the artistic, delicate ivy leaves, growing all over her cottage in delightfully random patterns, when her door swings open. "You better have a damn good reason why you're here," she croaks.

I look up, finding her wrinkled face inches from mine. Her pale green eyes assess me like a science project that's long overdue. "Hello, Georgina," I say, smiling innocently.

She bares her yellowish teeth, hissing like a cat. "Why are you here, Melissani?"

God, she's ancient. Sort of like Stonehenge, but less charismatic. I have a hard time focusing on my mission when she's glaring at me like she's about to shove me in the oven to turn me into roasted Melissani garnished with potatoes and beans.

"Melissani," she thunders. "Are you deaf? Why are you here? In my woods?"

Sweet baby Hekate, I have to get a grip. She's the only one who can help me, and I doubt eyeing her like she's the living, breathing example that some of us witches walked right out of a rather unpleasant fairy-tale is going to help much. "I…" *Pull it together!* "I'm here because I need your expertise," I say, begging the universe and every god and goddess ready to listen she won't turn me away.

"My expertise?" Georgina arches her gray eyebrow. "Is that so?"

I swallow the lump in my throat and nod. "It's important."

"And why would I help you?" the ancient witch asks, a wicked smile playing on her lips. "Your blood is tainted, Melissani." She crosses her arms. "And you know how I fare with the likes of you."

Why is it that everyone has to rub my screwed-up DNA under my nose, lately? Do I wear an invisible "My existence is flawed" tattoo on my forehead? Doesn't matter. I only have one shot at convincing her and I intend to make it count. "You've heard of the witch that killed legions?"

"I have," Georgina admits.

"Well, that would be me."

The old hag eyes me skeptically. "Is that so?"

"Yup."

She bites her lower lip. "Tell me, Melissani, why would a half-breed like you go about killing her own kind?"

"They're not my kind." I snort as rage ignites a low burning fire in the pit of my stomach, the same fire that's responsible for the demise of hundreds of demons.

Georgina tsks. "Nonsense. You are as much demon as you are witch. Therefore, they *are* your kind, too."

I want to burn the witch's face off and hang her skull next to the cat's just to prove a point. I'm not stupid though. Killing another witch wouldn't just put me on the red-list of the witch community, it would also attest to what Georgina said—that I am no different than the demons I slaughtered. I am, though. Demon blood or not, I'm nothing like those bitches. Besides, I still need Georgina's help. "Maybe so," I reply, having a hard time keeping the fire blazing inside me under control. "But my kind or not, I'm going to end this war once and for all. But…I can't do it on my own. I need your help."

"End the war?" Georgina's laughter echoes through the dark woods. "And how are you planning to do that?"

I nod at her door. "I'm sort of cold."

She hesitates but eventually caves and invites me in. "You've got five minutes."

More than enough time to convince her of my superior plan. "Thanks."

Chapter 7

*Leviathan*

"*If you refuse, I will end you.*" The boss' words echo through my mind, playing on repeat like a broken record. He honestly wants me to kill her and I…Lord in Hell, why did I even ask him what would happen if I refused? I've known him all my demonic life. I've seen how he trades with demons, daring to disobey him. The prime example? Her father. The idiot thought he could get out after she was born. I remember the day he approached the boss, asking him to strip his demonic powers so he could live out his remaining days raising his little family. (Why anyone would voluntarily give up their demonic existence to become human again will forever be a mystery to me.) The request was stupid and naïve, but it shouldn't have ended with the death penalty. That's exactly how it ended, though. And the boss didn't just kill him. No, that would have been too easy, too quick, too merciful. He used her father to set an example for any demon dumb enough to break the rules. His screams could be heard in the deepest and darkest parts of hell and they lasted twenty years, before one of the demons, tasked with torturing him, finally ended his misery.

Disobeying the boss has never been an option.

*It will never be an option.*

Why did I consider it, then?

*Because you're an idiot.*

An idiot? Could an idiot have played nations? Could an idiot have created a soul empire? Could an idiot have acquired such power? Of course, not. I'm smart, smarter than most. Which is why I would never disobey the boss, even if that means I have to kill her.

"Lev!" Berith seizes hold of my five-thousand-dollar leather jacket and pulls me back. "What do you think you're doing?" She and Verin followed me out of the meeting like two lost puppies treading on the heels of their master. Contrary to what humans believe, I actually like dogs. They're loyal and obedient little buggers. My siblings, however, are loyal but not obedient, otherwise they would have listened to me when I told them to get lost.

I cock a brow, tired of having to explain myself. "Let go, Berith." She might be my sister (the boss adopted her and Verin around the same time he adopted me) and most of the time I can tolerate her, but after everything that went down, I'm not in the mood to deal with her or anyone else for that matter. Not when the beast inside me demands blood, Abbadon's blood specifically.

She shakes her head, silver-blonde curls bouncing off her shoulders. "First, you have tell me what you're up to."

"Since when do I owe you an explanation?" I draw a deep breath, swallowing the rage rushing my system. "I am the—"

"Crown prince of hell," Verin grumbles, waving me off. "We know, man. But lately…"

I narrow my eyes at him, not liking where this conversation is headed. "What?"

"Nothing." He shrugs. "It's just…You haven't acted the part since you met her."

Oh, no. Not again with the nonsense. I've had a bad enough day. I really don't need a repeated sermon from the prince of impatience on how he's worried I suddenly discovered I have a heart. Because I don't. Have a heart, that is. Sure, there's a muscular organ beating in my chest, but it lacks love, compassion and all those other disgusting emotions humans so long for. Emotions my own brother is accusing me of. "She's just a witch."

Berith sighs. "Not to you she isn't."

My head snaps in Berith's direction. "What are you saying, sister?"

She averts her gaze, eyeing her new Manolos, instead. "I think…I think, you know what I'm saying."

"No, I don't." Me—Lord Satan, I can't even say her name. So, she might have been a mistake, but she wasn't my first one, and she most definitely won't be my last. (Yes, yes, I know what you're thinking. How can someone so awesome and perfect make mistakes, right? Well, I'm demon enough to admit that I might have a little weakness for pretty redheads. Especially if they are full of fire.) "And quite frankly," I continue coolly. "I don't understand what all the fuss is about. I bedded a witch. She couldn't get over the word 'goodbye' and now I have to kill her. End. Of. Story."

Verin shakes his head at my statement. "Keep telling yourself that, brother." He sighs. "But we know you."

"You didn't just bed her," Berith adds. "You felt something for her."

I laugh so hard my belly aches. "Have you lost

your minds? I'm a demon. I don't have feelings." Well, except for the sinful ones, of course.

Verin doesn't buy a word. He knows me too well, sometimes better than I know myself and I don't like the things his golden eyes imply. "Then why ask the boss what would happen if you refused to kill her?" Again with that question? Wasn't it enough that my own mind plagued me with it? Now I have to hear it from Verin, too?

I close my eyes and gather my wits. Why did I ask? What was I thinking? Did I think at all? The answer hits me like a bolt of lightning. "Because," I say, yanking my eyes open to face him. "She isn't just any witch, remember?" She is one of the most powerful creatures I have ever had the pleasure to come across. Half demon, half elemental witch—the hellfire in her soul could burn down nations. "Killing her is a damn waste."

Berith bites her lower lip, eyeing me carefully. "So, you are going to kill her?"

"Of course." What choice do I have? It's either her or me and I treasure my existence.

Verin laughs. "I'd like to see you try."

"Watch me succeed," I shoot back, walking away from them and the abhorrent mansion that ruined my day. My whole century.

## Chapter 8

*Melissani*

"Drink," Georgina orders, pointing her bony finger at the herb infused tea sitting on the dark green coffee table next to me.

"It could be poison," an insidious voice whispers in the back of my mind. I wouldn't put it past Georgina to kill me right here in her living room, where she keeps jars holding human hearts on a chest of drawers. But the curiosity in her gaze tells me, she is looking for answers. Answers only I can supply. So, I assume she won't kill me. Yet.

"Thanks." I reach for the steaming mug to take a sip.

"My pleasure." She nods, then folds her aged hands over her lap and says, "Tell me, child. Why would someone like you kill demons and talk about ending the war?"

*Someone like me, huh?* Meaning the daughter of a witch who broke the rules. A witch who screwed a demon and spawned a half-breed, who spawned me—an abomination as the late Lord Mammon called me so endearingly. "Name one elemental-witch who doesn't want this war to end?"

She flashes me her yellowed teeth and I can't help but wonder if they don't have dentists around this area. Georgina could surely benefit from seeing one. "I cannot do that, but you knew that already."

Of course, I did. The war between elementals and demons has been going on for half an eternity. It's even older than Stonehenge-Georgina and there's not a single elemental-witch who wouldn't give an arm and a leg to see it end. Our kind has suffered enough at the hands of demons and any witch with a grain of brain would do anything to end the witch-hunts and the cruel murders of our kind by the hands of those creatures. "That answers your question, then?"

"It doesn't." She cocks a brow. "And since you came to me begging for help, I suggest you speak your truth or be gone."

Goddess above, do witches like Georgina always have to be so difficult? Is it an age thing? Do we get crankier with age? If so, it might be a good thing I'm not planning on growing old. Wouldn't want to end like good old Stonehenge-Georgina. "It's a long story."

Georgina leans back, letting her head rest against the fluffy cushion embroidered with a bunch of cat faces. "I ain't got nowhere to go."

No? And here I thought she's about to go off in the woods to lure gullible children to their deaths. But no such luck it seems. "Fine." It's not like I have much of a choice. Georgina won't help me unless I spill my guts and I need her help if I ever want to see Faith again. "I assume you've heard of my mother?" She nods and gestures for me to continue. "Well, as you might know, she wouldn't win mother of the year and raised me quite…" *Hm, what's the word?* "Unconventionally?"

"That's one way of putting it."

Truth be told, it's the nicest way of putting it and I still can't quite believe how all of this started.

****

The light in the dining-room was still on, but the house eerily quiet. It didn't surprise me. According to my phone, it was quarter past three in the morning. Mom and Faith were either out and about to find a new victim they could talk out of his money, or they were upstairs getting some beauty sleep. I hoped for the latter, but with those two one never knew. Over the last two years, they had acquired quite the taste for scamming poor bastards out of their lifesavings by promising them love and happiness. How else could we have afforded a place like this? In a fancy neighborhood, surrounded by pediatricians, lawyers and all sorts of other respected professions? We couldn't have. Period. And while I appreciated the luxury that came with it, I loathed the fact that my seventeen-year-old sister was playing tricks on men. It had changed her. Changed her so much, I barely recognized her sometimes. The sweet, innocent girl, who used to pester me until I played with her, wasn't so innocent anymore. And instead of playing with dolls she now played with older men. Sometimes, I thought it had become some sick game of competition between her and Mom. Who could seduce the richer, the higher-ranking, the better man? It drove me nuts. But there was simply nothing I could do about it, except get a job as a bartender to show Faith that money could be earned honestly. Since I made half the money in a month that they made in a day, I was doing a piss poor job at setting a better example.

I made sure I'd locked the door behind me and kicked off my heels. I couldn't do anything about Faith and Mom, but I could surely do something about my groaning belly.

On my way to the kitchen, I passed the dining room and almost suffered a heart-attack as my mother's voice roared through the hallway. "Melissani?"

I stuck my head through the doorway. "Mom?" She sat at the table, her eyes oddly puffy. "Is everything okay?" I asked, slowly moving into the room. "Is Faith—"

"Faith is fine," Mom assured me, keeping her gaze on the piece of paper lying on the table in front of her. "But we need to talk." There was something odd about her voice, something that sounded a lot like despair. That was impossible, though. Because my mother didn't even know how to spell that word.

On edge, I approached the table. "What is it?" I would have added: *Can't it wait? Some people have an actual job and they're tired after a double shift.* But her rigid posture and her pallid face shut me up.

Mom snatched the piece of paper from the table, crumpled it and shoved it into the pocket of her tight, black pencil-skirt. Despite the ungodly hour, she looked like she had just emerged from the cover of a fashion magazine. "Sit," she ordered.

If I hadn't been worried before, I was now. "Mom, you're freaking me out. What happened?" The last time I'd seen her like this, we ended up moving halfway across the world over night.

One second Mom's eyes were soft and full of regret. The next they were cold as ice, reminding me why other witches had given her the pet name Ice Witch. It had little to do with her affinity for the watery element and everything with her cold, cunning demeanor. "I need you to do me a favor," she said.

"A favor?" The edge in my voice was obvious. Can you blame me? The last time she had asked for a favor, I became a murderer. Yes, it was a demon. But still.

She straightened her skirt and nodded. "It's important that you hear me out before you throw a tantrum which will be of no use, because at the end of this night, you will agree to my terms."

Right then and there, I learned the origin of the word terror. It started with fear and quickly turned into deep-rooted paranoia. One that begged me to run. I stayed and fucked-up my life instead. Story of my life.

\*\*\*\*

I push the unwanted memory away, ignore the toxin in Georgina's voice and move on. "Anyway, she introduced me to a demon and I..." I swallow the lump in my throat. "I made the mistake of trusting him."

"Trusting him with what, my dear? Your chastity?" Her laughter roars through my bones, chilling my insides. " 'Cause from what I've gathered, you shared a bed with the crown prince, Melissani."

I flinch at the weight of the truth, but it's too late to turn back. I need to see this through for Faith's sake. "I did and now I'm paying the price."

Georgina shifts to the edge of her seat, watching me like a hawk. "And what price would that be?"

My heart clenches so badly I fear I might die of a damn heart attack right here in this godforsaken cottage. And considering my luck, I'll turn into a damn ghost, forced to haunt these woods, adding yet another tale to the urban legends surrounding this area. "They...He..." *Just spill it, already!* "He took my sister."

Georgina cocks a brow. "The earth-witch using her

gifts to play tricks on men?" she says, her tone laced with revulsion.

"Faith isn't like that," I hiss. "It's just that my mother…" I shrug. "I told you, she wouldn't win mother of the year, didn't I?"

Georgina sighs. "Our parents might shape us, but we are responsible for our actions, my child. You'd do well to remember that."

I ignore her statement and move on. "Anyway, I'm trying to get Faith back."

"By ending the war between our kind and those abhorrent creatures?" She draws a deep breath. "I'm sorry, but I fail to see the connection."

I ball my fists, counting to three to keep my wrath in check. "There is a connection."

Sadness creeps into Georgina's expression. "Even if you're right and even if you can end the war and bring her back, you of all people should know that nobody returns from the pit unharmed. Every single soul…Well, hell changes them."

Changes them? I almost burst into laughter. That's a nice way of saying they turn into demons. I know that. I just don't care. No matter what my sister is I won't let her rot in the pit. I just can't. "Why don't you leave the consequences to me? I'll deal with them when the time comes."

"Nothing good can come out of this." She snorts.

"You're wrong." I put the mug back on the table and meet her gaze. "I've already taken down more demons than I can count. And if everything goes as planned, I will shut down the gates of hell for good."

Interest flares in her pale green eyes. "And how are you going to do that?"

"Easy." I flash her a brilliant smile. "I'm going to kill Leviathan and use his blood to seal the gates."

Understanding flickers across her stunned expression. "The hell-fire spell?"

I nod. "Yup." The very spell that only a half-breed like me can perform to close down hell for good. At least, that's what the legend says. And boy, I have never wished more for a fairytale to be true than in this case.

"And why do you need me?"

"Because I've tried to draw Lev out of his hole." I walked into bars full of demons, burning them to the ground before they even realized what was happening. I abducted his favorite warrior-demons, torturing them to the point where I wondered if I still had a soul, but the coward stayed hidden. "He never showed and obviously, he won't answer my call," I explain. "But he will—"

"Answer mine," she finishes for me.

"That's the plan."

"A silly plan."

"Maybe," I reply. "Maybe not."

She rises to her shaky feet. "I assume there's only one way to find out, huh?"

My eyes light up. "Does that mean you'll help me?"

She pulls me to my feet, ushering me to the door. "Come see me tomorrow night."

Tomorrow night, huh? I could wait till then. I'd spend every second plotting Lev's end. A cruel, inhuman end, I might add.

# Chapter 9

*Leviathan*

It's official: my siblings are morons! Seriously, they're so stupid it hurts. Taking the previous conversation into account, I'd go as far as to say they weren't around when hell provided brains.

"Killing her won't be easy," Berith had repeated time and time again. "You can't just pretend she's any other witch. You spent a goddamn year with her for fuck's sake."

"I could do it," Verin suggested. "I don't mind strangling the bitch."

"You can't," Berith said. "If the boss finds out, he'll toss both of you in the deepest and darkest part of the pit, feeding the keys of your cells to good old Cerberus."

"He doesn't need to know," Verin argued. "And it'd be my genuine pleasure to kill that stupid—"

"Enough!" My glass had finally been filled to the point where all my anger flowed over the rim.

Aware of my uncontrollable temper, Berith's eyes widened with fear. "We're just looking out for you," she said, in justification of their stupidity, but I was done listening to them. There was only so much stupidity a demon with my intelligence could take and the two had exceeded the limit by far.

"Get out!" The beast inside me pounded against

my ribcage, begging me to let it out. And I would have if my siblings hadn't been smart enough to run for their pathetic lives.

Now, hours later, I'm still sitting at my kitchen counter wondering why those two morons thought I would risk my own handsome, well-trained butt by disobeying a direct order from the boss to spare her life. Didn't they know me at all? Had they forgotten about all the empires I had destroyed in the course of history? About the countless souls I'd collected, the uncountable numbers of idiots I'd coerced to hell? How dare they question me. Questioning my loyalty and my need for self-preservation. How dare they think I felt anything other than pure lust when faced with those stunning, green eyes of hers. I mean, I won't sit here denying her hotness. In all of my existence, I'd never lain eyes on a more beautiful woman—be it witch, human, or demon—than her. But just because my fingers itch to run through her silky, red thatch doesn't mean I've forgotten who...No, what I am. I am Leviathan, the Prince of Envy, Ruler of 777 infernal regions and the Crown Prince of Hell. And I, sure as the impending apocalypse, am not in lo—I can't even say the word without washing my mouth with a shitload of disinfectant.

*Whatever. Let the morons think what they want.*

I've never given a second thought about anyone's opinion. And I surely won't start now. I've got more important things on my mind—like how am I going to get close enough to kill her?

*Kill her...Kill her...Kill her*—the most annoying echo ever, the words ring in my ears. Why though? What in the name of all unholy sinners is my problem?

Yes, Melissani Douke is a force to reckon with. She is one of the few beings with the power to end my superb existence with nothing but a single spark of hellfire. But—

*But you don't fear her, do you?*

I don't know. Do I?

*Or is it something else entirely that you fear?*

I don't fear. Period.

*Oh really? Then why are your hands trembling? And why is your heart cramping, huh?*

My hands are not—I look down...They're trembling all right. It must be the bourbon. And no, demons can't get drunk. That's beside the point though.

*Is it?*

For the love of Satan, can thoughts not be silenced? Would it help if I run the butcher knife, across from me on the kitchen counter, through my brain? Probably, but it'd ruin my vessel and then I'd have to find a new one, which is quite hard these days. All those hipster dudes are impossible. This whole mess does serve as a reminder of how much I hated self-reflection and I haven't done much of it since I shed my pitiful human skin. Which brings me to the realization that the last time I felt so pathetic I was still human. Yes, the crown prince of hell, contrary to all beliefs was once human. Most demons were. How? Well, that's sort of a long story. One equally disturbing and insane as its biblical equivalent in the book of Genesis and I won't bore you with the nasty details. I've got more pressing matters to attend to. One matter specifically: Killing Melissani.

"Lev?" Sala's voice draws me out of my own head. "Lev, you here?"

"Kitchen," I grumble, downing bourbon

number...two hundred? Or was it four hundred? Ah, who cares? Not me. The stuff doesn't work anyway.

Sala's high heels click against the marble floor announcing my assistant's entrance in one, two... "You won't believe what I just heard," she says on three.

Sala's purple eyes gleam. The demon has been assisting me for six decades. She's smart, loyal, and always gets the job done. She's basically my employee of the year. The downside? She loves gossip to the point where she invested a lot of time and money in creating the world's most notorious gossip magazine, which quickly got its own tv-show. Yup, that gossip-show you watch daily is the invention of a demon. Shocker, huh? "I'm not in the mood, Sala."

She tosses her rainbow-colored fishbone-braid over her shoulder and grins. "Sure about that?"

"Yup." The last thing I need is for her to share the newest who-is-screwing-who-in-hell news.

"My bad." She leans against the kitchen counter, grabbing the bottle to pour herself a drink. "I mean, I really thought you'd like to know your girlfriend is plotting with another witch to conjure your sorry ass."

My head snaps her way. "What did you just say?"

"Your girlfriend?" she grins.

I narrow my eyes at her. "Sala!"

Sala smiles like the devil she is. "Melissani is trying to conjure your pitiful ass to end you, my friend."

"That's perfect," I yell, jumping to my feet.

Sala looks at me as if I've just cuddled a scorpion. "Did you not hear the part where she's trying to conjure you to...You know, kill you?"

"I did," I say, flashing her my most charming grin, the one that made Cleopatra squirm. "And it's the best news I've heard all day."

"Did you lose your fucking mind, Lev?" Sala downs her shot. "You've been hiding from her because she's crazy, totally bonkers, and has lots of juice. If she manages to conjure your ass—"

"Oh, she will manage to conjure my *hot* ass," I say. "Unfortunately, she won't live to regret it."

"What are you doing?" Sala asks as I reach for my phone, dialing Berith's number.

"Getting ready to be conjured," I reply like the crazy but still awesome demon I am.

Chapter 10

*Melissani*

The human heart is a peculiar thing. The cardiac muscle is about the size of a closed fist and looks nothing like the heart a girl draws around the name of her crush in her notebook. If I had to compare it to anything, I'd go with a cone of soft ice with the point of the cone pointing down to the left. Yeah, it's an odd comparison but true, nevertheless. Another thing a heart and soft ice have in common? Frozen they can withstand a lot, but when they melt...They make a bloody mess. I should know. It was my melted heart that got my sister dragged to hell. But I've learned my lesson. My heart can no longer create a mess. Because like the one I'm starring at, the one floating in a jar of pink liquid on Georgina's shelf, I have separated mine from my body, refusing to allow it to influence any of my actions.

Actions like killing the monster I once thought I loved.

What a stupid witch I was.

But there's no point dwelling on past mistakes. What's done is done and soon—my gaze darts to Georgina, who's gathering a candle and white chalk for the conjuring spell—I'll get a chance to rectify at least one of those mistakes. Because let's be serious for a moment, I should have burned the obnoxious creature the instant he agreed to my mother's deal. Luckily, I'll get another shot. Thanks to Georgina.

Had I asked any other witch to call upon the crown prince of hell so I may torture and kill said prince, they would have laughed their asses off before they tossed my ass out of their houses. Not that elemental witches have a problem using black magic to conjure a demon. Nope, elementals don't differentiate between black and white magic. (We also love to see demons suffer and they suffer greatly when they're magically forced to do an elemental witch's bidding.) Anyway, our gifts are tied to the goddess Gaea also known as Mother Nature, who, according to our beliefs, also created those bitches—you know, to keep the balance, the natural order of things and that crap. Looking at the grand scheme of all things, it makes sense. Yeah, folks love to pretend the world is black and white, but the truth is the world was created in a million shades of gray and at the end of the day, it comes down to perspective. A murderer is a murderer? I don't know about that. Because what if it's a desperate mother pulling the trigger, ending the bastard who abused her daughter? Would folks be as quick to judge her? Or is their judgment reserved for those whose perspectives on life don't align with their own? I mean, don't get me wrong. I hate demons, hate them with a fierceness that allowed me to burn the flesh off their faces while they were still alive. And boy, did I enjoy their screams, their pain, their desperation. I bathed in their misery to the point where I questioned my own sanity. But I can't…No, I won't pretend demons aren't necessary. Every living and breathing creature was created with purpose. Even those bastards. Yet here I am, waiting for Georgina—

the only elemental who hates demons more than I do and therefore willing to participate in my madness—to draw Leviathan's sigil on her wooden floor, so she can summon the asshole.

"Are you sure this is what you want?" Georgina asks, eyeing me suspiciously. Almost as if she expects me to change my mind.

I force a smile I don't feel. "Why wouldn't I?" Lev abducted my sister and there's nothing I won't do to get her back. She's everything I have, not counting the mother who sold my soul. Yup, literally. She sold my soul and worse...I let her do it. But hey, life is too short for regrets. Especially when the afterlife ticket will take you straight to hell.

Georgina lights the white candle. Sitting cross-legged on the floor, she reminds me of an ancient yoggi, who mastered the art of eternal living by greeting the sun on a daily basis. "You might be able to lie to yourself, child, but I can see right through you."

The witch is annoying as fuck and rather skilled when it comes to bringing out my fire. But I need her, so I swallow my rage and smile like the good girl I used to be. You know, before I turned into...This. "I'm not paying you for a reading, Georgina."

"This one's free," she replies, meeting my gaze. "You may tell yourself that you hate him, that he's nothing to you, but we both know that's not true, don't we? And buried emotions aren't strength, they're a weakness which the enemy will most definitely exploit."

The only emotion I feel when I think of Leviathan is pure and utter disgust. It wasn't always like that. Once upon a time, I...I trusted him. Hell, whom am I trying to kid? I loved the prick. My stupidity was without precedent because, despite my better judgement, I pictured a future with him. Don't get me wrong, I knew who and what he was when I climbed into his bed. Leviathan's reputation preceded him, but I allowed myself to be blinded by his charm, his wit, and his lies. I don't know what I was thinking, but I blame the save-the-bad-boy syndrome for my poor life choices. "Thanks for the unwanted advice." I point to the burning candle. "Can we do this now?"

Georgina straightens her spine and looks up at the ceiling. "I draw my power from earth," she chants, her voice like honey. "I follow the divine rules of the creator. I do as I want but harm none. Ye who created all things, I call upon thee, bring forth what my heart seeks." She reaches for the paper with Lev's name written on it and holds it over the flame. "Leviathan, son of Beelzebub, I call upon thee. Open the door and come through to see me."

The walls of Georgina's cottage rattle as the ground beneath my feet starts shaking. I fist my hands, digging my sharp nails into my skin. I dig so hard I draw blood.

*This is it! This is payback!*

I have waited for this moment, longed for it, for so long and I know…I know, I should be thrilled, should be fucking happy, but—

Cold sweat dots my palms and my heart races like the treacherous monster it is. Not in anticipation but in…Wait, is this fear?

*No!*

I cured myself of fear. I shed it like a snake sheds its skin, remember?

*Then why are you shaking?*

Because…Because I was so wrapped up in my need for revenge, I'd never taken the time to consider what it would feel like to face him once more. All I ever allowed myself to think about were a million ways to end him. I was going to be his reaper and a reaper didn't care about inhumanly bright emerald eyes, nor did the kiss of death require a touch of his full bow-shaped lips. I didn't care if he would look at me like he used to— like he was in hell, and I was his path to salvation. But now…Now I'm—

*You're what? Stupid! Jesus, Melissani! Who cares about his eyes? About the way he once looked at you? He's a fucking liar, remember? He crossed his heart and then he broke his promises. He watched you suffer and made you feel like you deserved it. He didn't just break your heart. He tore through skin and bone and ripped it from your goddam chest. And then, when it lay on the floor, damaged and broken beyond repair…What did he do then, huh?*

He abducted Faith and dragged her to hell.

*And now? What are you going to do about it?*

I draw a deep breath and smile. "And now I'm going to kill him for it," I whisper.

On cue the bastard's voice thunders through the cottage as he materializes next to Georgina's altar, dressed like a goddamn rock star. "Hello, my love."

Goodbye my love would have been more appropriate.

# Chapter 11

*Leviathan*

So, you think demons like my stunning self are evil, huh? Well, have you ever been conjured by a demon in the midst of taking a bubble bath? No? That's what I thought. I'm telling you, finding yourself butt naked in a protective circle on some remote crossroad in the company of a stupid human, who believes fame, fortune, or the attention of another human (sometimes a combination of all three) is worth an afterlife of torture and pain is appalling. It makes me nauseous, too. Luckily, I have an amazing assistant, who managed to give me a heads up this time, giving me a chance to prepare myself for the unpleasant trip. What it didn't prepare me for is the bitter-sweet hatred flooding the cottage when Mel spots me. "It's been a while," I say, flashing her a surprisingly easy smile.

She wears ripped black jeans, a white heavy metal band shirt and her favorite sneakers. Not much has changed about her dressing habits since we last stood face to face. Her demeanor, however, is nothing like it used to be. Arms crossed, she glares at me like I'm the source of all her nightmares. "Not nearly long enough," she retorts, the edge in her voice sharper than I remembered.

"So hostile." I shake my head and laugh. "Where are your manners, love?"

"They're reserved for those who deserve them," she shoots back.

The salt line of the magical circle separates us, but the distance isn't enough to spare me from the hard-core hate washing through her system. I have no clue what happened to the little witch, but the last time I saw her, it wasn't hate that radiated from her.

\*\*\*\*

*I moved quietly into the living room where Mel waited for my return from what was supposed to be my last business meeting ever. She sat on the sofa, hands folded in her lap, gaze glued to the small suitcase sitting on the hardwood floor beside her. She was deep in thought, didn't even hear me coming, which gave me a moment to drown out the stupid voice in the back of my mind, the one that kept saying,* You can't do it. It will ruin her.

*I took a deep breath and tossed the keys into the oval-shaped wooden bowl, which Mel got me a couple of weeks ago, because I kept misplacing my keys. It wasn't that big of a deal for me. Demons didn't necessarily need keys to enter a house or anything else for that matter, but Mel insisted. She had put the bowl on the sideboard next to the entrance and I hadn't lost my keys since.*

*"Lev?" She looked over her shoulder, smiling at me like I was some kind of hero rather than the villain who had bought her soul.*

*I wanted to return the smile, but I couldn't, and it wasn't because I had suddenly grown a heart like my brother accused me of two hours ago. What didn't sit right with me about this was I would have to break the promise I made to her. A silly, delusional promise. A promise, nevertheless. Why did the crown prince of hell care about breaking a promise? Well, it had little to do with a guilty conscience and everything with honor and integrity. Demons deal in promises and our success as well as our reputation depends on making true on them. But this one, this one I should have never made.* "Hey," *I finally said.*

*One look was all it took.* "What's wrong?"

*Us. Together. That was what was wrong, and I needed her to see that. That stupid voice, though, it messed with my resolve.* Don't do it. You will regret it.

*No! I would not regret it. Mel and I had a good time, we enjoyed each other, but what was it the boss always said?* "Pleasure has an expiration date. Make sure to remember that, or else you will end up upsetting your stomach." *He was right, and in that moment, I wished I had checked the date sooner rather than later.*

"Leviathan?" *Her voice shook with a foreboding kind of fear.* "What happened?"

"Nothing."

*She studied me.* "You're lying."

"I'm always lying." *I was a demon. It came with the job description and Mel should have known that by now. Except, I had never lied to her. Until now. Guess, it was true. There was a first for everything.*

*She rose from the sofa and took a step toward me, brushing against the suitcase. It fell, emptying all of her belongings on the hardwood floor.* "Shit." *She kneeled to clean up the mess.*

*It was the perfect moment to crush her hopes and dreams.* "When you're done with that, I want you to leave."

*She looked up.* "What?"

I pointed at her clothes. "Pack your stuff and leave."

"But..." She sighed. "You still have to pack your stuff."

I swallowed the odd, sour taste of poisoned lemons and made sure my impenetrable, cold as a fish mask was in place. "And why would I do that?"

Confusion clouded her eyes. "What do you mean? I thought, we're going to—"

"You shouldn't think," I cut her off. "Pretty heads like yours aren't made for that."

She abandoned her clothes and walked right up to me. "Lev, what's going on?" The trembling in her voice wasn't the only indicator of fear. I tasted it on the tip of my tongue and every step in my direction left her more afraid. "What happened? Talk to me."

I wouldn't go down that road. Not then. Not ever. So, I simply crossed my arms, and said, "I'm done with you, little witch."

"You're what?"

"We had a good ride, but it's time to change the horse." Satan, I hated that analogy. Mel wasn't a horse. She was the most beautiful thing I'd ever had and giving her up...It did something to me. Something I couldn't quite comprehend or explain. But it was necessary.

The pain washing through her system left my mouth dry. Weird. The pain of others usually tasted like strawberries not like old socks from the lost and found section of the Sahara. "You said we'd run. Together."

"I'm a liar, remember?"

"No." She reached for my hand, but I pulled back. "You..." She found my eyes. "Why are you doing this?

*What happened, Lev?"*

*I couldn't explain myself. Neither could I stand her sadness any longer. It made me feel weak and pathetic and I was neither. I was the crown prince of hell, and I did not cave or change my ways for a witch. "Leave, Mel." I walked to her suitcase and loaded it up. "Leave this place and don't ever come back."*

*She tried to stop me, tried to pull the suitcase away from me, but I was so much stronger than her. "Stop!" I let the darkness shine through my eyes, warning her. "We are done," I said, voice cold. "Now, the way I see it, you've got two options." I pointed at the door. "Get out of here and enjoy the remainder of your life before I claim your soul and add it to my collection. Or"—I looked into that ocean of green, forcing an evil grin— "stay and I will collect what's mine a little early."*

*She glared at my chest. Thick, black smoke slowly pushed out of its prison, oozing through my pores. My darkness grew fast, spreading like shadowy tentacles of an octopus out to hunt its next prey. And while she was fearless and brave, she was also smart enough to know I didn't mess around. I never messed around. "You mean that, don't you?"*

*I handed her the suitcase. "I do."*

*"Maybe—"*

*"The next time I see you I will collect what's mine," I cut her off, not in the mood to hear what stupid reasons she had to stay despite my warning. "Did I make myself clear?"*

*A sad smile curled her lips. "Yeah," she whispered, tears filling her eyes. "You did."*

*She walked away and despite everything, she did so gracefully with her head held high and her shoulders straight.*

*The instant the door slammed shut behind her, I released a breath and whispered, "Until we meet again, love."*

****

"I've got to admit," Mel says with a sharpness I've never heard from her, one that shatters the memory of the broken girl that walked out of my apartment and replaces it with the image of a witch, who burnt an entire castle (inhabitants included) to the ground. "I'm surprised you had the guts to crawl out from beneath the rock where you were hiding." Every fiber of her is infected with hate. A hate so fierce it snakes around my neck, choking the wits out of me.

*What the ever-loving hell happened to you, Melissani?*

I drink her in. She's still as mesmerizing as the day we first met. Cat-shaped green eyes, wavy red hair, curves to die for—she's walking sin, born to drive demons like me into blissful, obsessive madness. And her beauty isn't even the most attractive thing about her. What truly defines her, differentiates her from all the others, is the way she carries herself, like she knows who she is and what she wants, and nothing could ever come between her and her goals. Don't get me wrong. She has insecurities. I still sense them on her, but she never tried to cover them up. She comes as she is as I always want her to be—a lover, a friend, a woman, a witch, an enemy. So, yes, she's hot on the outside, but what gets to me is the spitfire in her eyes. "It would be a shame if someone as handsome and intelligent as me hid under a rock, don't you think, love?"

I assume aggravating her further isn't my best idea.

She does have the power to kill me, after all. But it's too late to reminiscent about the past. Mel has already lifted her left hand, allowing the hatred to bring forth a lush flame of green hellfire. "You shouldn't have come," she whispers, turning the flame into a ball and aiming the fiery projectile at me.

I grin like the cute demon I am. "Guess, you shouldn't have asked good old Georgi to call upon me then, love."

It takes a second, but then something shifts in her gaze. "Georgi?" she parrots. Her gaze shifts from me to the old hag.

Georgi sighs heavily. "I'm sorry, child." The meaning of her words is lost in translation, until I hold my hand out to help good old Georgi to her feet.

Mel's jaw is unhinged. "What the—"

"What you're planning to do would upset the natural order," the old hag says to justify her treachery. "And no matter how much I hate those bastards, I cannot stand by and watch you destroy our goddess' creation. Hell is needed and you know it, Melissani."

Melissani—or Mel as I used to call her—is about two seconds from using the fire-projectile to send good old Georgi to her grave. "You...You played me!"

"She did," I say. The intel about Mel trying to conjure me didn't just drop into Sala's lap. It was good old Georgi herself who gave Sala a heads-up, because she feared Mel's plan might be successful. The old hag hates us, but she'd sell her own child to uphold the natural order. "Hasn't your mother told you?" I add fire to the fuel. "Never trust a witch."

Georgi lowers her gaze. Shame colors her wrinkled face deep red. "I had no choice."

A heat wave bursts through the living room. "One always has a choice," Mel whispers, throwing the ball of pure hellfire at the old witch.

A single high-pitched scream escapes the hag's throat before she turns into a pile of bone-dust.

Whoa, someone might want to sign up for an anger management class. And that someone is not me. Careful not to ruin my shoes, I step over what's left of Georgi. "That wasn't very nice," I say, slowly advancing toward her, ignoring the protective salt line that may hold lesser demons, but certainly not the crown prince of hell.

Another ball of hellfire appears in her palm. "Wanna see how nice I am?"

I flash her a crooked smile. "I think I know all about your niceness." And while it might have come out sarcastic it wasn't meant to be. Melissani used to be the kind of girl that helped strangers in need, saved kittens from trees…Yada, yada, yada…You get the picture, right? So annoying!

Her gaze narrows. "Still a cocky bastard, I see."

She holds the hellfire in her hands. I shouldn't provoke her but bringing out her worst is fun. "Still a high tempered bitch, I see."

"What can I say?" She lifts her hand, ready to turn all of my decadent hotness into ashes. "I do enjoy the heat."

The gleam in her eyes alerts me that she really is going to toss that thing at me. Too bad she didn't follow my advice. "Hey, Mel?" She glares at me. "What did I tell you about watching your six?"

Like a cobra, her head snaps back, but it's too late. Berith is already behind her, grabbing her arms and slamming iron shackles around her delicate wrists.

If I had a heart, I'd feel sorry for the beautiful witch. Being played and cornered like this must be a terrible disgrace. But being sentimental isn't exactly an attribute bestowed upon hell's future ruler. "You've got two options, love."

"I take death," she spits at me, even though she has no clue which options I planned to offer her.

Berith sighs dramatically. "She truly is something," she says, echoing my first impression of Melissani. The one branded into my brain.

**** 

*The pulsating beat of the music vibrated through the packed bar. I had just dealt with a rogue reaper working for a New York based Striga to collect souls ahead of their expiration date when I stumbled across the fancy bar, one favored by the who's who of Famous-Town. Rich kids, actors, and musicians frequented the bar, where everything was on the menu—waitresses and cocaine included.*

*Since the reaper hadn't gone down without a fight and ruined my favorite pair of ripped jeans, I wasn't in the best mood. I just felt like drowning my anger with lots of bourbon and minding my own business, when a strawberry-blonde woman approached me. "Leviathan?" She all but whispered my name. Not out of fear or respect, though. It was more like she wanted to make sure no one overheard her.*

*I studied the middle-aged woman for an instant and thought her high-cheekbones and the pouty mouth looked familiar but couldn't quite place her. "Not interested," I murmured, downing another shot of bourbon.*

"But you are," she said, pulling a chair to the table and sitting her butt down, even though I didn't invite her. (So rude! No manners whatsoever!)

I could smell her need. It tainted the air and made me wish I'd never worked the crossroads in the first place. Sure, it had been a long time since I had struck deals with mortals, but the memo—I'm done making deals—hadn't spread far enough yet. "Whatever you want the answer is no." I eyed my empty glass. "So, why don't you go find some low-level demon. He'll surely be happy to strike that deal."

The woman laughed then. "A low-level demon?"

"Is that funny?"

She nodded. "Yes, it is."

My interest was piqued. "How so?"

She inched closer. "See, what I have to offer…" She smiled. "Well, let's just say a low-level demon wouldn't be so low-level anymore if he got his hands on it."

All right, I was officially curious. "And what could that possibly be?"

"The soul of my daughter," she said with an easiness that made me question her sanity.

I laughed. "The soul of your daughter?" Did she confuse me with Rumpelstiltskin? "I'm honored you think I'm so rotten that I'd take the soul of your daughter without consent. Truly am. But there are rules, laws even I have to abide by."

"You're the crown prince," she said, gaze narrowed. "If anyone can bend the rules it's you."

Pride bloated my chest, and I appreciated her vote of confidence greatly. However, even I had standards and accepting a third-party's soul as a bargaining chip *wasn't something I was willing to do. So, yes, I was about to send this sorry excuse of a mother back to whatever hole she'd crawled out from, when I caught sight of a petite redhead with bright green eyes. She was stunning. Her pale skin was flawless, her cat-shaped eyes breathtaking, and the glow around her...It had a magnetic pull that drew my attention and didn't allow me to refocus. In a bar full of supermodels, she stood out like an alien from planet* Special. *And it seemed I wasn't the only one who recognized her otherworldliness. One of those rich kids, a preppy boy reeking of dad's money, rocking the boring boy-next-door-turned-model look walked up to her.*

*He bent down to whisper something I couldn't hear.*

*Whatever it was, though, wasn't appreciated by the beauty. Quite the contrary. She turned around and laughed at him. "You're delusional," she barked, her deep laughter vibrating through my bones like the beat of the music.*

*I knew it was rude to stare at the strange girl while I had a potential customer offering the soul of her daughter, and I was raised better than that. Yet, I couldn't take my gaze off her. Her purple shirt with a famous band logo and her ripped jeans didn't fit in, but she didn't seem to care. She still carried herself better than any of the other girls in the bar and her grace... It was without precedent.*

*"You think you're special?" the preppy boy barked and this time I had no problem hearing him, he was loud and rude.*

*The girl smiled then. "I don't think I'm special."*
*She shrugged. "I* know *I'm special."*

*That was all it took to bring out the demon buried in the human's soul. One second, he looked at her dumbstruck, the next he grabbed her and pressed her against him.*

*I don't know what got into me then, but I rose to my feet, ready to show the rich boy whose demon was bigger and more bad ass.*

*I made it two steps before I saw the girl's devilish grin. "Bad life choice," she said as green flames sparked in her eyes. A heartbeat later, the flames pulsated through her hand. The very hand that had grabbed preppy-boy's wrist.*

*His screams were pure pleasure to my ears and when the scent of burned flesh wafted through the bar and his fingertips were literally on fire, I knew... I just knew I had to have her.*

*I walked up to her about to introduce myself when my potential customer appeared by my side and said, "Leviathan, meet my daughter." She pointed at the pouting girl. "Melissani, the only hellfire witch alive."*

*Yup, I was smitten. There was something about a girl that held her own, a girl that had the power to do so much more than just burn rich boy's fingertips off. I knew right then and there I needed her soul. So, I agreed to that stupid deal, and the rest...Well, the rest is ancient history.*

\*\*\*\*

"Yes," I agree with my sister. "She is something."

"Something stupid." Verin grunts, guarding the entrance to Georgi's cottage.

Melissani's gaze darts from my siblings to me. She isn't nearly dumb enough to believe she can get out of this mess unharmed. She's powerful, but not powerful enough to take all of us out while the iron around her wrists messes with her powers. "Do it," she yells. "Kill me. I've got nothing left to lose. There's nothing that you haven't taken from me."

Verin takes a drag from his smoke. "C'mon, Lev, you heard her. End it. I mean, she's practically begging, isn't she?"

She is and that strikes me as odd. Melissani is a lot of things, but she isn't one to give up easily. Where is her spark? Her fight? Her stubbornness? And what did she mean when she said I took everything from her? What did I take that she didn't willingly offer? Not her body. Not her mind. And surely not her heart. "Tell me," I hear myself say. "Did you cause all that carnage just because I broke your heart?"

Melissani throws her head back and laughs heartily. "My heart? You think this is about us? About you being a fucking coward?"

"Careful how you speak to him," Verin warns.

Melissani glares at him. "I will speak to him however the fuck I want, asshole. He isn't my prince, remember?"

Verin snorts and I see he's two seconds from unleashing hell on her, so I step between them. "Tell me, love." I make the grave mistake of looking into her fiery eyes. They're laced with so much pain it tugs at the heart I don't have. "If you didn't piss off the boss and all of hell because I kicked you out of my bed, then why?"

Her laughter sounds crazy and I'm starting to fear for her sanity. Like maybe we should call a shrink or something. "I can't believe you!"

"What the fuck is she talking about?" Berith asks,

as if I have a clue what's going on in that crazy head of hers.

I shrug. "No idea."

"Fucking liar." A burst of heat floods the cottage, reminding everyone present just how strong Melissani truly is. If we lose focus, she could do something stupid, like use her powers despite the iron around her wrists, blowing all of us—including herself—to hell.

"Let's just kill her and be done with her," Verin says.

Berith nods. "Hate to say it, but Verin has a point."

"Enough!" I'm done listening to their unwanted advice and I'm done playing Melissani's games. I stalk toward her, stopping inches before her. "I am a liar," I say proudly. "And the king of heresy, but as of right now I'm also very confused. A state of mind I don't exactly treasure, love. So, why don't you do me a favor and tell me what it is you think I did apart from saying goodbye."

"Go to hell," Melissani barks, spitting on the floor.

I smile like the nice guy I'll never be. "Not very imaginative." I wrap my fingers around her neck, feeling her vein pulsate under my thumb as I apply just enough pressure to block her airway. "So, let's try this again, shall we? What did I do?"

"Fuck you!" Melissani is way too proud to cave, and I was betting on it, because I enjoy holding her like this. It reminds me of—Never mind.

"That wasn't very lady like," I whisper in her ear, rubbing my thumb over her throbbing vein.

"I never said I was a lady," she retorted.

"I know. What I don't know is why you went out there wreaking havoc. So, one last time, tell me what you think I did, or I will—"

"Kill me?" She laughs. "I'm counting on it. Because I'd rather die than see your ugly face any longer."

I should snap her pretty neck and be done with her, but something holds me back. And that something will surely get me into a lot of trouble with the boss later. But right now, I just don't care. "Sleep," I mutter softly, allowing my darkness to infiltrate her mind and her soul.

"Lev," Verin barks as I catch Melissani's limp body before she hits the ground. "What the hell are you doing?"

I lift her and open the portal we came through. "Finding out why she's lost her damn mind."

Berith blocks my path. "That's a bad idea, Lev. You ought to kill her not abduct her."

"Yeah," Verin hisses. "What if she kills you first?"

I look at her angelic face resting against my chest. "She won't."

"Tell that to poor Georgi," Berith murmurs, glaring at the pile of ash.

"She betrayed her," I say, passing through the portal. "And paid the price for it." A pretty high price. One that the old Mel, the one I knew, would have never requested. But people change and apparently witches do, too.

Chapter 12

*Melissani*

I'm floating on a black cloud, slowly carrying me through the starless night sky. Lev's magic put me here. His scent is all over the place. It smells like a thunderstorm brewing in a star sprinkled summer night and brings forth memories I'd rather forget.

\*\*\*\*

*I looked up at the night sky, wondering why my own mother sold me off like cattle. Did she care so little about me? Did she not love me at all? She hadn't always been like that. I remembered a time when she tucked me in bed and told me stories about fearless warrior princesses destined for greatness. Sometimes, we spent hours watching silly TV shows, laughing, and joking about the weird characters. She had been a good mother back before my sister was born, and we moved to the States. Whatever happened changed her in ways I could never fully comprehend. And as of now, I was too tired to even try to make sense of the mystery that was my mother. It was also too late. What she'd done, what I let her do...* Goddess above, why did I sign that stupid contract? Did I care so little about myself? Didn't I have an ounce of selflove and self-respect? *It—*

*"It's beautiful, isn't it?" His chilling voice cut through my thoughts.*

*I didn't need to turn. I'd recognize his faint British*

accent anytime, anywhere. Well, it was sort of hard to forget the voice of the demon prince who bought your soul, wasn't it?

Why did he follow me? Did he come to gloat? To make fun of the stupid witch who sold her soul for her mother? A mother who hated her enough to ask her to give up her soul so she could gain more power? *"I'm aware my soul is yours now, but I'm still alive, which means I still get to make my own decisions and I came here to be alone."*

He sat down beside me, ignoring my wishes, and gazed up at the stars. "That's Cassiopeia," he said, pointing at a V-shaped constellation, which connected to a vertical and horizontal line.

I sat still, not moving an inch, not saying a word. It would have been pointless. Men like him didn't care about a woman's wishes. They didn't understand the concept of "no" and too often they lived by the motto: No means yes.

"She was a queen," he explained, paying little attention to my balled fists and my rigid posture. "A proud and vain one, who considered herself the most beautiful woman of all. Her arrogance didn't sit well with Poseidon and so he sent a sea monster to kill her."

I hated him, couldn't stand him, but I also wanted to know whether Poseidon succeeded and why her arrogance bothered the god so greatly, but I couldn't bring myself to ask. The demon had just bought my soul for crying out loud. I didn't need mythology lessons from a guy who had no honor and certainly no conscience.

"Her husband, King Cepheus, couldn't just let her die," he continued as if he sensed my curiosity. "And *so, he begged the gods for help. They answered his prayers and told him that in order to save his wife he must sacrifice his daughter to the monster." The prince shifted closer, his warm breath caressing my cheek. "He chained his little girl to a rock and left her to be devoured by the sea monster."*

*"I sort of know how that feels," I murmured.*

*The demon prince laughed. "You do, don't you?"*

*I cast him a sidelong glance and kept my mouth shut. Mostly because I didn't think he'd appreciate the insults waiting to be unleashed.*

*He put two fingers under my chin and with surprising softness he turned my head, so we were face to face. "Perseus saved the girl," he finished the story. "And even though you might not believe it just yet, you are safe too. Because I treasure what's mine, Melissani." The second our gazes collided I caught sight of lightning forking through the sky. The air was thick. Electrified. The scent of a brewing summer storm wafted between us. "Always."*

*I wanted to blame Stockholm syndrome for the warmth spreading in my chest, wanted to attest my racing heart to fear, but that would have been a lie. Because as I was sitting there underneath the constellation of a rotten mother, who had gladly sacrificed her own daughter, I realized losing my soul wasn't my biggest problem.*

\*\*\*\*

I had kept those rare happy moments locked away in a box that I never intended to open again. A box I only kept because I wanted to remember how it felt to be cherished, something my own mother failed to teach me. Something a demon—the damn crown prince of hell—taught me, instead. There was a time I would have done anything for him, a time when his kisses meant the world to me. But our past can't outweigh the present. What we had…It's over. And there's no point dwelling on it, not when the bitter and ugly truth is sinking its claws into my heart. Lev played me. Ruined me. And the second his spell fades, the instant I'm able to move my sleeping limbs, to open my damn eyes, he'll pay for his sins. Like Georgina paid for hers.

*Be patient, Melissani. Just be patient. It's—*

"He will have your damn head for this," a familiar voice cuts through my thoughts.

"Don't be a drama queen," Lev says, sounding amused.

"A drama queen?" his sister barks, sounding eerily worried for a demon princess. "You disobeyed a direct order, Lev. You think he's just going to be okay with that?"

Who the hell is he? And why would he be dumb enough to go against Lev? The prick is the king of hell's favorite pet and no demon in his right mind would mess with him. Unless—

"Berith is right," Verin adds. "If the boss finds out you didn't kill her, he will have your head."

*The boss? As in his father? The fucking king of hell?* No, that can't be right. Lev is a selfish prick, who doesn't play by anyone's rules. Except for his father's. He would never disregard his orders, no matter what.

"Chill," Lev barks, obviously not short on temper. "He gave me three days, remember? I haven't broken any rules." He pauses to add a quiet, "Yet."

The spell he's put me under must mess with my hearing because I could have sworn, he said, "Yet." But that's impossible. Verin and Berith would be throwing fits had he implied what I think he did.

"Help me out, man." Berith sounds really desperate at this point. "Why would you take her home if you're planning to kill her?"

*Yeah, Lev, why would you? Better question: Why the fuck did I ever think I could trust Georgina?* I should have known better than that. Even my mother had warned me about the old hag. What was it she had said when I called her to ask for the witch's whereabouts? Ah, yes. "Are you crazy, Melissani? I understand you want to save your sister and while I condone your violent deeds of the past few weeks, I do support your search and rescue mission. But...Georgina? All the old witch cares about is upholding the natural order. She would sell her own child if it fit her purpose." I thought that was rich, coming from a woman who sold the soul of her first-born daughter to a demon, but in hindsight, I might have been better off had I listened to mommy-dearest for once.

There's a long pause, then Lev says, "I'm curious."

"Curious?" Verin spits back at him. "Father is going to kill you because you're fucking curious?"

"He won't kill me," Lev replies with a certainty that rattles my bones. "Sure, if I don't kill her, he'll be mad. Maybe he'll toss me in the frozen wasteland for a while. But..." He pauses. "He would never kill me. He needs me to keep his empire running."

"Anyone is replaceable," Verin shoots back. "Even you, brother."

Lev laughs. "Have you eaten a clown for breakfast?"

"I'm serious," Verin murmurs.

"So am I," Lev retorts. "See, no one can replace me. I am unique and—"

"Your pride is going to be the death of you," Berith says.

"The death of us," Verin says.

"No." Berith exhales sharply. "Because Lev will kill her."

Silence.

"Lev," Berith yells. "Tell me I'm right. Tell me that you will kill her!" Berith sounds like she's pleading. It doesn't suit her.

Lev doesn't answer. Instead, he barks, "I think I have put up long enough with the stupidity of you two! So, why don't you get the out of my apartment and make yourselves useful by grabbing some witch-hazel for me."

*Witch-hazel? Are you trying to poison me, prick?* And here I thought he'd come up with a more imaginative way of killing me like spooning my heart out or skinning me alive. Guess, I overestimated him. Again.

"You're fucking crazy," Verin mutters, before a door slams shut, leaving me alone with my worst nightmare.

Chapter 13

*Leviathan*

I never quite understood the hype about watching someone sleep. Not only did I think it was weird that girls on one hand, wanted to be watched in their sleep, but on the other, constantly filed police complains when someone was stalking them (so contradicting), it was also incredibly boring—even for someone with my abilities, someone, who could enter dreams. (It was like watching reruns of a soap opera—love, lust, betrayal...You get the general picture, right?) Yet despite all that, I lean against the door frame and stare at sleeping-witch-beauty.

She's shackled and tied to a chair. There's no sign of distress. Her breathing is calm and relaxed. Her body at ease. She looks so peaceful, almost like one of those small angel statues people often leave on the graves of their loved ones. You know, the one resting its head on its forearms, looking like they don't have a care in the world.

*She is no angel, though.*

No, no she is not, and I know better than to underestimate her unbreakable spirit.

\*\*\*\*

*"Have you lost your mind?" I yelled at her.*

*She drew a deep breath and shoved the letter in the back pocket of her jeans. "No, Lev. Have you?" she asked, her brow arched.*

*I couldn't remember the last time someone dared to ask me such an insulting question. My sheer presence put the fear of Satan in demons and humans alike. But Melissani? She's impossible. Impossibly stupid. "I won't let you go!"*

*She laughed.*

*"I don't see how any of this is funny."*

*"It is," she says. "Because it almost sounded as if you think you get a say in where I go or what I do."*

*My darkness banged against my chest, begging me to let it out to show the witch that I did have a say in everything she did. "I own your soul."*

*"When I'm dead," she shot back.*

*"I could kill you right away," I said and partly meant it. Melissani drove me crazy, and she had the ability to stretch my patience like no one else and I dealt with the worst humanity had to offer. (Try to reason with a man who wants to extinguish a whole ethnicity within a few days and I'm sure you'll get what I'm saying.)*

*If she had been right in her head, if she had an ounce of self-preservation, she would have crumbled in fear. But Mel wasn't right in the head, and she had no idea what the term self-preservation meant. "Go on, then." She opened her arms as if she were going to hug me. "Kill me."*

*"Mel," I said as a warning, barely able to keep the beast inside me under lock and key. "This invitation could be a trap." Maybe I could reason with her. Maybe she could—*

*"I don't care," she replied.*

*"Come again?"*

*"You heard me." She crossed her arms. "Even if it is a trap, I still need to go. They won't murder me at my sister's initiation."*

*"Says who?" I would have totally murdered someone at her sister's initiation.*

*Mel rolled her eyes. "The witch codex, Lev."*

*"The same witch codex that brands you as an abomination?"*

*I saw the very instant I lost that fight. The moment the spark of hellfire gleamed in her eyes. "Look, you can either kill me or watch me leave." She smiled like the sun. "Which one is it going to be?"*

\*\*\*\*

Since she's currently tied to a chair, you might be able to guess who won that fight. It was also the first time I've ever caved. Ugh, not exactly my best of days. But Mel has that certain something, a fire in her soul that's not just tied to her magic. It's tied to her personality. Witches like her are the reason my father came up with the law in the first place. The one that says: No Screwing Around With Witches. It wasn't always like that. There used to be a time when demons and elemental witches like Mel got along just fine, sharing spells and bodily fluids. But the elementals grew tired of being used by us and when the uproar started, they used their charisma and sexuality to turn some of us. Quite a few of my demonic brothers lost their minds back then, claiming they'd found love and purpose, when in reality they were simply subjected to the witches' spells. I mean, every demon child knows we don't have hearts. Sure, we obsess over certain things, kind of like human stalkers do, but we never, and I mean *Never* fall in love.

Despite my siblings' claims, I'm not a fool. I won't spare Mel's life just because we had something going. The witch will die and her soul—my soul, thanks to her mother—will be a treasured trophy in my collection. First, however, I need to know why one of the smartest witches I know is acting like a brainless zombie.

Placing my hands on the arms of the chair she rests in, I lean down, savoring the scent of lavender and jasmine. I take several inhales before I lower my lips to her ear and whisper, "Wake up."

She blinks open her breathtaking eyes. For a moment, I forget who I am and what I want. Then I spot the gleaming hate in her gaze and draw back.

"You should have killed me," she says, smiling devilishly.

Calm and collected, I wink at her. "And you should have known better than to slaughter legions of demons."

"Why?" A lopsided grin tugs at her full lips. "Did I upset your daddy?" She tries to move her hands, but quickly realizes they're still encased in the iron shackles. Not being able to burn me alive doesn't stop her from spewing her venom, though. "I heard he's giving you a hard time. Man, I'm so *not* sorry."

Melissani's stab-worthy mouth is one of the things that made me turn my back on the no-screwing-witches-rule. She can't just raise hell with that mouth, she turns a demon with no heart to brainless pudding if she uses it the right way. And the thought of said right way wakes my best friend, who hammers against the zipper of my jeans, wanting to be let out to play. "You haven't changed one bit."

"You're wrong," she says.

I shake my head. "I'm never wrong." (I'm better than that old hag of Delphi when it comes to predicting the future. It's why she forbade me from entering her cave. Jealousy can do that to the best of us. Not me. I'm never jealous. Why would I be? I am the best.)

"Yeah?" She arches a brow. "Then take off these shackles, and we'll see about that."

"I'm not nearly stupid enough to fall for your madness, Mel." She'd burn my ass without hesitation. "And since I'm on a clock, I'd appreciate it if you'd tell me why you've gone all red-haired-super-spy-assassin on my men."

A flash of anger mixed with hurt flickers across her eyes. "As if you don't know."

"I don't," I admit. "And you know how much I abhor being kept in the dark."

"Liar," she mutters, averting her gaze.

I draw back, taking a deep, calming breath. "That I am, and I appreciate the compliment, but I still don't know why you've lost your mind, love."

A shaky laugh escapes her. "Yeah, right."

"What is wrong with you, Mel?" Can't she see that I'm trying really hard to take the high road instead of ripping off her beautiful head? "You know I'm a liar, but have I ever lied to you?"

"Yes," comes her quick reply.

"When?" I ask. "When did I ever lie to you?" *Except once and you can't know about that. Or else we wouldn't be here today.*

"When didn't you?" she retorts, driving me up the wall.

"Look," I say, leaning down to her mouth that practically begs me to claim it. "I don't want to make this harder for you than it has to be, and I don't want to bring you unnecessary pain," I whisper, focusing really hard on my father, hoping it'll calm the beast (the other one in my pants). "But I can, and I will hurt you."

She shrugs. "So, do it."

Doesn't she know better than to challenge me? Hasn't she witnessed what happens to the ones that did before her? Is she stupid or just suicidal? Either way, I can't pull back from my threat. In hell, reputation is everything and if someone finds out I used empty threats, I will no longer be the most feared of them all. "As you wish," I say, allowing the darkness inside me to break the surface. It only takes a second for my power to find the cord, connecting her soul to my essence. Then it seeps into her, searching for her most painful memories and experiences and once it finds them, it pushes them to the surface and amplifies the pain they once brought her.

Melissani's screams bring me no joy, no pleasure. Instead, they make me sick to my stomach, make me question my own selfishness. *I don't care about her. I don't care about her. No, I revel in her pain. I—*

"Talk!" I yell, barely able to keep my anger in check. *Satan, what has become of me?* Maybe I should join those "How To Be More Hateful" classes Verin suggested.

"No," she whispers, tears streaming down her cheeks.

"Please," I say, wiping her tears away. "Please, just tell me and I'll stop."

But Melissani doesn't cave and deep down I already knew that. "Pain is life," she chokes out, swallowing another burst of unfiltered pain created by the memory of her mother selling her off in that fancy NYC bar. "Hurt me all you want, but I won't tell you shit."

"We'll see about that," I hiss, rolling the darkness back into my gut and walking the fuck away from her before I end up doing something stupid like kissing or killing her.

Chapter 14

*Melissani*

The pain in my chest is still fresh when Berith and Verin return with the witch-hazel. They take one glance at my smeared mascara and grin like they won the fucking lottery. "Someone was enjoying himself," Verin says cheerfully.

Berith rolls her eyes. "Shut up, Ver."

But Verin keeps smiling like a happy camper. "C'mon, don't act as if you aren't worried about his sanity." He tilts his chin at me. "At least now we know he can still torture the fuck out of someone."

"I might as well torture the fuck out of you," Lev says, walking out of his bedroom with a bottle of bourbon in his hand.

*Has he been drinking? Come on, Mel. Mr. I-don't-use-that-sort-of-language just said the f-word, what do you think?*

"Go, prepare the witch-hazel potion," he orders, eyes cloudy.

*Yup, he has been drinking and judging from the looks of it this isn't his first bottle.* The metabolism of demons works differently. They need a whole lot of juice to get tipsy and I'm fairly certain there isn't enough bourbon in the state to get them drunk.

"You heard him," Berith says, ushering Verin out of the living room and into the kitchen. "Let's get the potion ready."

"Whatever," the bastard grumbles.

Lev moves toward me, eyeing me like a damn hawk.

"I know I'm pretty, but that doesn't mean I enjoy being stared at."

Lev sighs. "And what do you enjoy, Mel?"

"Watching you burn," I reply.

"Obviously," he says, taking a swig straight from the bottle.

"So, while dumb and dumber try to prepare a useless potion, you might as well tell me, since when has the crown prince of hell turned into an alcoholic."

Smiling, he holds the bottle under my nose. "Why, want some?"

"Nah." I shake my head. "Looks like you've had enough for the both of us."

He brushes a loose strand of hair out of my face, gently securing it behind my ear. "So judgmental."

"Not judgmental, *Your Highness*. Just stating facts."

Lev inches closer. I feel his fiery, bourbon breath on my forehead. The organ in my chest hammers against my ribcage like the treacherous beast it is and there's nothing I can do about it, except hate myself a little more. Not an easy task considering I'm barely able to look at my reflection anymore. "Why couldn't you enjoy the life you were given?" he asks, running his thumb down my neck along my throbbing vein. "You could have had happy years, Mel. You could have grown old with some worthless bastard, having kids of your own. And then, once you died peacefully, we would have been reunited and you could have been the princess you were born to be." His harsh laughter ripples through my marrow, sending chilly waves down my spine. "But you just had to go and fuck it all up, didn't you?"

"I fucked up?" I glare at him in utter disbelieve. "Are you so self-absorbed that you dare put this on me?"

He draws back, meeting my gaze. "Who else would I blame?"

"Yourself, you asshole."

He studies me carefully, trying to find a loophole that would allow him to penetrate my armor, but there's none. Whatever I once felt for him is gone. Gone like my sister. "What happened to you, Mel?"

"You," I spit back at him. "You happened to me."

His lips part, but Berith cuts him off. "It's ready," she announces, holding up a steaming pot.

"Good." Lev rises to his feet. "Let's find out why little miss sunshine turned into a wicked witch, shall we?"

## Chapter 15

*Leviathan*

I retrieve the steaming pot from Berith's grip. "Last chance," I warn her. "Tell me, why you slaughtered all those demons, and I swear, I will grant you a quick death."

"You swear?" She laughs hysterically. "I've learned the hard way that your promises don't mean shit, Lev. So, why don't you spare me the meaningless chatter? Besides"—she eyes Verin, who grins like the idiotic demon prince he is—"I'd rather spend eternity being tortured by your goons than to tell you anything."

Why did I ever think Mel would play by my rules? Ah, right. I didn't. Deep down, I always knew she'd rather die than do what I say. Maybe I should have tried reverse psychology on her. Maybe she would have voluntarily spilled the beans had I asked her not to. Or maybe I'm just delusional and you know what they say about illusions, right? Reality never quite lives up to them. And this reality is...Not my cup of tea. But what can I do? A job is a job. "Hold her down," I order Berith.

Verin moves instead. I stop him. "Stand back." This will be painful enough I don't need him to hurt her even worse.

Berith grabs her head, pulling it slightly back to give me access to her mouth. "You could have prevented this," I remind her before I force the potion down her throat, careful not to overdose and accidently kill her before I get the answers I crave.

The witch-hazel, toxic to elementals, works quickly. In a matter of seconds, Mel's body twitches and jerks as if she's sitting on the hot chair, being electrocuted. Tears stream down her cheeks. She doesn't scream though. She's too proud for that.

"She could use a little more," Verin suggests innocently.

I ignore him and wait for the potion to settle in her soul. When Mel stops twitching and her head falls back, I know it's time. "Listen to me," I whisper, gently holding her face between my palms, while my darkness seeps into her mind, clouding her forest green eyes and eventually turning them black. "I need you to tell the truth. Can you do that?"

She nods.

Witch-hazel when used correctly won't kill an elemental, but it will open her up for demonic compulsion, and so I allow my darkness to infiltrate every cell of her brain. Then, I draw on the cord connecting us and use my softest and most convincing voice. "Tell me, why did you kill those demons?"

"Because I wanted to draw you out," she mutters.

That much I already guessed. "Why?"

"To kill you," she says.

"Why would you want to kill me?" I can think of a million reasons, but I need to hear it from her.

She laughs. "Because you lied to me, you betrayed me."

"I never lied to you." *Except once.*

\*\*\*\*

*It had been three weeks since Mel had walked out of my apartment. Three weeks which felt like an eternity of misery. I had somehow gotten used to waking up next to the witch, had gotten used to claiming her whenever the need hit. Now I needed distraction and thank Satan the boss had tasked me with quite a few jobs that required my expertise.*

*One of said jobs was currently tied to a chair in the middle of an abandoned warehouse. (Fine, it wasn't abandoned. The rats claimed it after production was shut down. Happy?) The guy—a lawyer working for a prestigious law firm in Washington DC—bled all over my shoes and I didn't appreciate it at all. It was so hard to find comfortable shoes, and these were my favorite pair. A pair I could toss in the trash after this, because there was no way the crimson would come off the white leather. "Please," he pleaded. "I didn't know he'd go on killing."*

*"That's a lie," I said, wiping the silver blade on his trousers. "And you know it."*

*He shook his head. "You're wrong. I—"*

*"I'm never wrong," I whispered into his ear. (It's why Delphi hated me, remember?) "See, I can taste your fear, can smell your lies and even if I couldn't, I'd still be able to see through your cheap charade." He was never going to win an Oscar, that I was absolutely certain of.*

*"I don't understand," he said, tears pricking his eyes. "You're a demon. Why do you care about his killing spree?"*

*"I don't," I admit.*

*"Then why torture me?" he asked confused.*

*Humans. They really didn't understand hell's*

system, did they? "You used a loophole to get him out of jail, knowing he would continue slaughtering children."

"So, what if I did?" he barked, anger flooding his system. "Demons kill all the time."

"Wrong," I assured him. "We collect souls and sometimes we plant a few homicidal thoughts to make the whole freewill game a bit more interesting, but that doesn't mean we go around slaughtering children. Especially if those children are potential customers." (Okay, yes! Sometimes we did kill. Mostly out of boredom but never children. Their souls were too important for both heaven and hell.)

"That doesn't even make sense," he hissed.

"To you it doesn't." I pushed the knife against his neck. "To us it very much does. Now, last chance. Tell me where he is."

"I—"

"I swear," I said. "If you say I don't know one more time, I will castrate you." (A practice I learned from the old Greeks. They were good at creating eunuchs. But please, don't start asking how they went from Sparta to castrating little boys. That story requires lots of alcohol and time.)

His eyes went wide, and the fear eventually crippled his resolve. "Lexington Road." He drew a sharp breath. "He's hiding at his girlfriend's place on Lexington Road."

I beamed at him. "Now, that wasn't so hard now, was it?"

He shook his head. "Can I go now?"

"Sure," I said, pushing the knife right through his miserable heart. "Enjoy the ride downstairs."

*I had barely wiped the dude's blood off my cheek when I heard her. "Still a liar, huh?"*

*For an instant, I thought I suffered from hallucinations, that I had gotten so used to Mel's voice that my stupid mind fell prey to illusions, but then she stood before me, eyeing the dead lawyer with a frown. "What did he ever do to you?"*

*"Long story," I replied, determined not to submit to the urge to pull her against my chest. "What are you doing here, Mel?" I narrow my eyes at her. "I believe I made myself quite clear when I told you I would kill you the next time I saw you, didn't I?"*

*"You did," she assured me. "But we need to talk."*

*"About what?"*

*"About us," she explained, her voice hard and unforgiving.*

*I turned away from her, straightening my shoulders. "There's nothing to talk about."*

*"There is," she said. "And I need you to hear me out."*

*I took a deep breath and faced her. "Go on then."*

*"I want my soul back."*

*I laughed. So loudly it shook the walls of the abandoned warehouse. "And I want Santa to hand out human hearts, but we don't always get what we want, Mel."*

*She sighed. "Look, I know for a fact you don't want to spend eternity with me, so I spoke to another demon, and he offered to make a trade with you. He'll get you the soul of another witch in exchange for mine."*

*"Another demon?" Who the hell would even dare to think about going behind my back? "And who would*

*that be?"*

*"Does it matter?" she replied. "He will give you any other soul in exchange for mine."*

*It did matter, because I felt like writing said demon a lovely letter in his own disgusting blood. "It doesn't." I smiled. "Matter, I mean. Because I will never give up your soul."*

*"Why?" She bit her lip. "You made it perfectly clear you don't want me anymore. So, why not give up my soul and spare yourself the prospect of an eternity with me?"*

*A million thoughts flashed through my mind, but I only gave voice to the one I could hold on to. "Because as greatly as the prospect of enduring you for the rest of forever pains me, I would never give up the kind of power your soul has to offer and any demon with a shred of brains should know that."*

*"You hate me," she barked.*

*"I do," I replied. "But that doesn't change the fact, I will gladly use you as my witch-slave, when the time comes." That said, I walked away and left her for the second time within three weeks, left her with a lie I knew I'd regret.*

\*\*\*\*

And here we are.

Her head jerks up, and she glares at me with an intensity that catches me off guard. "You have always lied to me. And now…Now Faith is paying the price for my actions."

"Faith?" Her sister? What does she have to do with any of this? "Why would Faith be paying the price?" And what price are we talking about?

"You know damn well why," Mel barks, her head

swinging left and right.

"I don't," I admit.

"Liar," she shoots back.

All right, I've had about enough of her accusations. Leaning toward her, I rest my palms on her cold cheeks. "Where is Faith, Mel?" I close my eyes and push deeper into her mind. "Tell me, where your sister is!"

Mel breaks into hysteric laughter. "Why don't you tell me where she is? You're the one who dragged her down to the pit, right?"

I pull back. The cord between us snaps. My darkness retreats. My mind reels. "I did what?" I yell.

Berith shakes her head. "Maybe she's gone mad?"

"Or maybe she was played," Verin of all people suggests.

I turn to him. "What are you saying?"

He leans against the door frame, watching Mel like a predator watches prey. "Think about it, Lev. She slaughtered legions, drawing the attention of the boss. And why? Because she's convinced you dragged her sister to hell? I thought she was just another love-sick witch, but now I'm wondering…"

"What?"

"If the both of you are being played."

"And why would anyone mess with me?"

"Because they want your spot at the boss' side," Berith answers. "And whoever is playing this game will win if you don't kill her."

My gaze darts to Mel. She's completely helpless. I could end her in the blink of an eye, but what fun would that be? "Sober her up," I order, walking out of the living room before anyone can question my sanity. Actually, it's too late. I am already questioning it.

## Chapter 16

*Melissani*

The instant I had sensed Georgina's betrayal, I knew how this story was going to end. Lev's reputation precedes him. The crown prince prides himself on never taking prisoners and he kills without hesitation. Which means, I should be pushing daisies right now, while my corpse is rotting in a sewer or some other rat-hole. He could have spared himself the trouble and ended my pitiful existence in Georgina's cottage, because let's face it: I am powerful, but when I spotted Berith behind me, I knew it was game over. So, yeah, my soul should now be a part of Lev's treasured and rather exotic collection and I should totally worry about the first assignment as his personal witch-slave. (Because that's what happens to witches who are dumb enough to strike a deal with hell. We don't go to purgatory like all the other scum, demons included. No, we are turned into slaves because no one told hell that slavery is no longer a thing in the modern world.) So, if I die, I'm bound to do the demon's bidding, his dirty work and as far as I know, there are no unions in hell, so employees don't get a vote.

But I'm neither dead nor off to wreak havoc in Lev's name. Because Lev...Lev didn't kill me.

*Why? Why am I not dead? Better yet, why didn't he kill me?*

The instant he poured the witch-hazel potion down my throat, I sent a last prayer to the gods and made amends with the fatal choices that didn't just screw up my life but my sister's, too. I came to terms with the fact I'd never get to avenge Faith's destiny, never get to save her from hell. Because I was going to die in the living room of the demon I used to cozy up to, the one who fucked me over. But…

I didn't die.

Why the fuck didn't I die? Lev should have whacked me, for fuck's sake!

Yet here I am. Tied to a fucking chair with the same iron shackles that held me down earlier, still…Still breathing.

*Why?*

My brain is too damaged to answer the question. The witch-hazel still messes with my mind, sparking tiny fires in the pit of my stomach threatening to burn everything in its vicinity to the ground.

*What's holding me back?*

The iron shackles slicing into my wrists.

*Are they, though?*

Iron shackles or not, I could end this once and for all, could end him by burning this place to the ground, leaving nothing but ash. The problem? I'd kill myself in the process because that's what iron does to witches like me. It works like a lightning conductor. The second I use my power the iron will toss it back at me. But if I used all my magic, the self-combustion would take down Lev's crib and anyone in it.

Why aren't you doing it then?

No fucking clue!

*Goddess, Melissani, you're so screwed.*

That I am. Lev kept me alive for a reason. One I surely won't like. The bastard is a selfish prick with masochistic tendencies, and I have a feeling I would have preferred purgatory to whatever he has up his sleeve.

*Only one way to find out, girl. Open your eyes and face whatever you've gotten yourself into. It'd be the brave thing to do.*

I'm not so sure about brave, but it's what I have to do.

"She's coming to," Berith whispers.

"Great," Verin grumbles, sounding less than happy about my consciousness.

"Melissani?" Berith's chilling red eyes meet mine. "How are you feeling?"

"What does it look like?" I shut my aching eyes, then blink them open again, hoping they'll adjust to the bright lights flooding Lev's living room.

Verin grunts. "Like you're in some real delicious state of pain."

"Asshole."

"Whore," he retorts.

I manage a lazy grin. "Wow, does your mother know you're using her profession as an invective?"

Verin glares at me like he's two seconds away from slicing my throat, but his retribution never comes. Probably because Lev walks in, looking all cheerful and happy. "Mel," he says, smiling like the boy-next-door he'll never be. "I'm thrilled you're finally awake."

The fire bursting through my veins, ignites my insides and if it weren't for the fucking shackles, Lev's stupid grin would be burned off his pretty face.

"We have a lot to discuss."

"We," I hiss. "Have nothing to discuss." Apart from his last wishes and the funeral rites he'd like to receive. I'd gladly pass them on to his father after I roast him.

He snatches a chair, pulling it across the wooden floor. The screeching sound drives me up the wall, like fingernails on chalkboard. "Don't be so grumpy," he says, putting the chair across from mine and sitting his fine ass down. "I have a feeling you'll like what I have to say."

"There's nothing I like about you."

"Oh, c'mon now, Mel. Don't lie." He flashes me an innocent smile, shifting closer to my ear. "I remember you liking me buried inside you. Doubt that has changed since we last had the pleasure."

The throbbing between my legs is a dead giveaway of how fucked up I truly am. Because as much as I hate Lev, he is right. I did like his hands on me. Hell, there was a time I thought I loved the way he pushed inside me, turning the fire in my veins into a full-blooded firestorm. And even though I hate him now with a fierceness that turned me into a demon-killing serial-witch-killer, I can't deny the effect his closeness still has on me. Yup, as fucked up as it is, part of me still longs for what we once had. But that won't stop me from killing him the moment I get the chance.

"Good Satan," Verin mutters through gritted teeth. "Can you guys stop the flirting? I can taste her desire and don't appreciate it."

"But I do," Lev says, running his hand up and down my inner thigh. "It still tastes like heaven."

I swallow the ball of emotions threatening to constrict my airway. "And how would a demon know what heaven tastes like?"

He inches even closer, tracing my jawline with his nose. "Like you," he whispers. "It's got to taste like you." The spark in his green eyes when he draws back, the way he rubs his palm up and down my thigh—good god it drives me crazy and all of a sudden, I'm grateful that these damn shackles hold me down. Because I can't tell whether I'd jump him or slaughter him right under Berith's and Verin's noses.

Berith waves Lev off. "Oh, for the devil's sake, get a room you two. Verin is right. I, too, can taste your longing and since I haven't had breakfast yet, I'd rather not."

The demons might be annoying as fuck, but they have a point. I need to get my libido under control. And I start by stating the obvious, "I'm still alive."

Lev leans back in his chair, withdrawing his hand. "You are."

"Why?"

"Because of your pretty smile?"

"Lev," I bark, just about done with his stupid games.

"Mel?"

"Answer the question?"

"Which one, love?"

"Why. Am. I. Alive?"

"Ah." He laughs. "That question. Well…" He pauses. "Would you believe me if I told you I just couldn't kill you?"

"No," I reply without hesitation. "So, why?"

"Because I like you?"

I've had it with the prick. "Leviathan." His name rolls off the tip of my tongue like thunder and lightning all at once. "Tell me, why the fuck you didn't kill me?"

He rolls his eyes. "Lord in Hell, you're no fun."

I narrow my eyes at him. "I might be tied to this chair with iron shackles, but I promise you, I will still find a way to burn you even if I burn myself in the process."

Lev finds my gaze and he quickly realizes I'm not messing around. "Fine. Have it your way, love."

"I'm not your love."

"No," he retorts. "But my dirty dream or my sex-slave doesn't sound half as endearing as love, don't you think?"

"Fuck you!"

"Hey, what did I tell you about foul language?" He sighs. "It's below you, Mel. You're better than that."

"I'm better when you're dead."

"But you'd miss me."

"I—"

"Enough with the sick foreplay," Verin cuts me off. "You're still breathing, because I think the two of you are being played and this,"—he glares at Lev—"fucker refuses to kill you before he knows who's playing you."

"Playing us?" I laugh so hard my belly aches. "Are you serious?" When I realize no one else is laughing, I straighten my back. "You are serious."

Lev nods. "Where is your sister, Mel?"

Unfiltered rage stabs at my heart, causing the flames inside me to spark even higher. "You tell me, Lev. Where did you take her?"

"I didn't take her," he says his voice stern and even.

"Yeah, right."

He leans forward, resting his elbows on his knees. "Melissani, look at me." I make the mistake and do just that. The price I pay for that stupid decision? I'm drowning in an ocean of liquefied emeralds. "I did not take your sister," he repeats slowly.

*He's a fucking liar! You can't believe a word he's saying! He's—*

"I'm a demon, Mel."

"Really? I thought you were a puppy."

He ignores my side-jab. "We lie and cheat, we betray and create chaos, but..." He reaches for the bone-knife. The one he got from his father after his first successful mission. The one he always carries in a holster at his back. "You know we are bound to our words." He slices the blade made of the remains of an upper-level-demon across his palm, drawing blood. "So, I, Leviathan, Crown Prince of Hell, give you my word that I did not harm your sister in any way. I did not take her soul, nor did I drag her to hell."

The instant the crimson hits the hardwood floor, burning a hole through it like acid, I realize what he's just done. A blood oath which means... "Y-you didn't take her?"

He shakes his head. "I did not, but I would like to know who did."

# Chapter 17

*Leviathan*

Melissani has never been the kind of girl to be rendered speechless. She always has a witty comeback ready to toss. She always has to have the last word. She never backs down from a fight and she surely has never looked at me the way she does now. Honestly, I feel like I died, came back as a handsome ghost and am now face to face with the girl I've been haunting in her worst nightmares. Because that's exactly how she looks at me. Her eyes are wide open, her jaw is dropped, and her skin is so ashen she too could be mistaken for a spirit. "B-but..." She shakes her head. "I thought you..."

"You were wrong," I grumble, not sure why it pisses me off that she thinks me capable of dragging her sister to hell. I'm a demon. I take plenty of souls to hell, or at the very least I make sure their choices secure them a one-way ticket to the pit. But her sister? Why in the name of Satan would I drag her to hell? Granted, Faith is annoying, and she hates me fiercely, but she's still Mel's sister. Besides, we have laws in hell. You can't just go around abducting witches or humans and taking them downstairs. Souls must be given to us voluntarily or they must be tainted due to some bad life choices. So, what was Mel thinking?

Mel's eyes are still clouded from the witch-hazel.

"I…" She swallows hard. "I don't understand."

Part of me wants to scream at her, wants to shake her until the witch-hazel is out of her system and she's capable of understanding the impact of her choices. Of her stupidity, really. Yes, she was stupid! I mean, she could have just called. I would have told her I had nothing to do with Faith's disappearance.

*And then? She wouldn't have believed you.*

No. No, she wouldn't have. (Occupational hazard since lying is part of my job description.) Still. She should have called me. Should have…I don't know. Anything would have been better than going all vengeful assassin on the boss' legions and winning herself a spot on hell's Wanted: Dead, Not Alive list.

"Neither do we," Berith says.

Verin cocks a brow. "Speak for yourself, sister."

Mel shifts slightly and looks at my brother. "Fill me in then."

Verin sighs. "Do you know why demons hate love?"

Mel frowns. "Because you're incapable of feeling it?" Ah, there she is. The witty witch is alive after all.

"Yes, but that's not the only reason." Verin leans against the wall, crossing his arms above his chest. "Love is like cancer. It's a damaged cell in your body that grows and multiplies when it shouldn't. And before you know it, it turns into a tumor, spreads into nearby tissue and kills you slowly but steadily."

"Wow." I stare at my brother in disbelief. "When did you study medicine?"

He shrugs. "As a young demon, I spent quite some time in hospitals. It's a good place for business."

"I'm sure it is," I say.

"Nice metaphor and all," Mel grumbles. "But I still fail to see how any of this connects to Lev, Faith or me."

Berith laughs. "Are you really that blind? Or just stupid?"

Mel narrows her eyes. "Stupid enough to burn this shithole down along with anyone in it."

"Go on and try." Berith inches closer, her posture rigid. "We'll see who's quicker, won't we?"

"Enough," I bark, not in the mood for a catfight. (At least, not today.)

Verin shares my sentiment and continues his explanation. "What I was trying to say is that whoever came up with the plan played on your love for my brother and you fell right into the trap."

"Love?" Mel laughs hysterically. "I don't love this"—she casts me a sidelong glance that could kill lesser demons—"prick."

"No," Berith says. "You hate him."

"Exactly," Mel barks.

Berith shakes her head. "You hate him, because you once loved him, Melissani."

"That's bullshit," she shoots back. "I—"

"You can only ever hate what you once loved." Berith leans down and smiles innocently. "But you already knew that, didn't you?"

Mel averts her gaze and all of a sudden, she's awfully quiet. Too quiet.

I'd rather handle a raving mad Mel than a silent one, so I bring the discussion back on track. "What they're implying is we were set up."

"By someone who counted on your temper," Berith says.

"And your need for revenge," Verin adds.

The remaining color drains from Mel's face. "Are you saying someone dragged my sister to hell because they wanted me to kill Lev?" She shakes her head. "Do you realize how crazy that sounds? I mean, why didn't they just kill him themselves?"

Did she seriously just ask that? "I am the crown prince of hell," I shoot back. "No one *just* kills me. Least of all a demon. They'd be insane to even try." All of hell knows what happens if you cross me. (Hitler knows, too. When in doubt they could ask him. Oh, wait. No, they can't. He's currently trapped in a Dybbuk, forced to spend the rest of eternity listening to glorious Jewish folklore and music.)

"Which is why they wanted me to do it?"

"So, you're not stupid, after all," Berith says.

Mel is all set to give my sister hell, but Verin is quicker. "That seems to have been the plan. But you failed, sweetheart, and now he has to kill you, or—"

"That's enough," I say, rising to my feet.

"Why? Let her know what her stupidity did."

Mel eyes me curiously. "What is he talking about?"

I flash her a smile. "Nothing, love." I face my siblings. "You two. Out. Now."

"But—"

"Now!" I yell, cutting Berith off.

They know better than to challenge my command and once they're out the door, I look at her. Really look at her. The girl with the soul made of hellfire looks shattered and broken, like an empty shell that'll soon be swallowed by the tide. It doesn't suit her. "Tell me what happened to Faith," I say softly, nudging her leg.

Mel's gaze darts over my shoulder. She avoids

meeting my eyes at all costs. Looks at the Venus painting on the wall, the Tang Dynasty vase on the shelf, the poster of the famous guitarist next to my hi-fi system—anywhere but my eyes. (Can't blame her. I have stunning eyes and you can get lost in them). "A couple of weeks after you…" She clears her throat. "Ended things, I went to see her. Her and Mom were trying to find their newest victim."

"So, Row is still hexing poor bastards for their fortunes?" I ask, not the least bit surprised when Mel nods. "Old habits die hard, huh?"

"Looks like it," she mutters, a fresh burst of pain and anger rushing through her system. I taste it on the tip of my tongue. It's like chocolate. Dark, bitter chocolate. A taste I don't enjoy as much as I used to. "Anyway, Faith was acting weird."

"Weird how?" I inquire, finding my fingers on her knee, drawing circles.

Mel shrugs. "She barely acknowledged my existence and I thought it was because…" She sighs. "Because of us."

"Makes sense." After Row—Mel's mother—traded Mel's soul for the powers of an air-witch whose gifts I had recently acquired, Faith had grown to hate me. For some reason, she'd decided to put the blame on me instead of her mother, who sold her sister's soul for a bit of magic. "Faith doesn't like me."

Mel laughs. A real laugh. One that touches her eyes and reminds me of binge-watching a senseless TV series and her ridiculous imitations of the actors. "That's quite the understatement, don't you think?"

"Probably," I admit. "But I'm practicing humbleness."

Mel cocks a brow. "Humbleness?"

I shrug it off. "So, what happened?"

A dark cloud washes over her eyes. "She simply vanished."

"She vanished and you thought I'd taken her to hell?" Sure, I'm an asshole. (Correction, a smart, handsome, and cunning asshole.) But abducting the sisters of ex-lovers isn't exactly how I earned my reputation as the most ruthless of them all. Besides, abducting girls is more Hades' métier.

"No." She shakes her head. "That wasn't my first thought, but when I did a locator spell and saw Faith in the pit, shackled and tortured…"

"You blamed me?"

She shrugs. "Who else would I blame?"

I can't believe her. "Do I look like I'm running a witch-trafficking ring?"

A spark ignites in her eyes. "You're a fucking liar, Lev. You used me, abused me, and then you tossed me in the trash like an old banana."

"Old bananas are the sweetest of them all."

"Can you drop the bullshit?" she barks. "I'm trying really hard not to burn us both to the ground and you're not making it any easier."

I lift my hands apologetically. "Sorry, my bad."

"Anyway, I figured I could draw you out if I burned enough of your bitches, but I forgot just how selfish you are."

"Don't confuse selfishness and self-preservation, love."

"Would you stop calling me that?"

"Why?" I ask, leaning in to sniff her remarkable scent. It's a mixture of wrath, hate and a whole lot of lust. "Does it bother you, *love*?"

"Go to hell!"

"Are we back to being unimaginative?"

She rolls her eyes. "I'm tired, Lev. I'm really tired. So, please, drop the bullshit, okay?"

Mel doesn't usually plead with anyone, least of all me. The fact that she just does, tugs at the heart I don't possess. "All right," I say, grabbing the iron key out of my pocket and burning my damn fingertips in the process. "I'm going to take those off now." I point to her shackles. "Will you try not to kill me?"

"Why?"

I sigh. "Because you need me to get your sister out of hell."

Her eyes go wide. "Are you..." She shakes her head as if she's trying to wake from a dream. "You are saying you'll help me?"

"I'm helping myself," I mutter unlocking the shackles. "Because whoever took your sister wants me dead, love, and I can't let that slide. You understand, don't you?"

"Selfish as always," she replies.

"Don't be a hypocrite, Mel." I rub my hands over her bruised wrists and smile. "You didn't complain about my selfishness when we rolled in the hay. You screamed my name in pure pleasure. So, don't start now."

Chapter 18

*Melissani*

When the locator spell tracked my sister to hell, I had sworn an oath to any god and goddess willing to listen. I was going to free my sister, kill Lev and use his blood to perform the legendary hell-fire spell, closing the gates of hell forever and ridding the world of all evil (myself included.) It all sounded so simple back then. Maybe it was my rage, the hate or just my damn pride, but I couldn't see myself failing. I had one goal and was ready to turn into a monster to achieve it. One simple goal and I...I screwed up royally. Why? Because Leviathan is still alive.

He's breathing and not because I lacked opportunities to off him. I had plenty of chances to end him—in Georgina's cottage, in his apartment and of course, when he took off the iron shackles. It would have been so easy to burn him to the point where even his father wouldn't have recognized him anymore. See, he might be the crown prince of hell and he's without a doubt one of the most powerful demons in existence, but I...I am something far worse. Georgina—may the old hag rot in hell—didn't lie when she claimed I was a half-breed. My mother's taste in men was as rotten as her parenting skills. That's why she got knocked up by a demon—the father I never wanted, never met either. Anyway, I was lucky or unlucky enough to inherit my mother's elemental magic—the fire—and my father's demonic DNA. The odd mixture created what the late Lord Mammon referred to as an abomination, otherwise known as a hellfire witch. Yup, that's my official title. I like it even better than Lady Melissani. It suits my style. No one knows what I'm truly capable of. Not the demons, not the witches…Jesus, even I have no clue how much damage I could inflict if I were to let the darkness, residing in a locked cage in the depths of my soul, out. In the course of history, there have been only a handful witches like me. Most of them were slaughtered shortly after they were born. Demons and witches joined forces to make sure those children never got to test their strengths. That's why my mother ran from her coven and raised me in England. She figured I'd be safe there. And I was. Or at the very least I survived until now. From the few things I dug up on hellfire witches in old grimoires and ancient writings, I learned the fire inside me is an extension of hell's ever burning flame, a flame that can kill any and all demons. So, yeah, I could have ended Lev and his pathetic siblings in a heartbeat. But…

*You didn't.*

No, I didn't.

*"Why?"* that annoying as hell voice in the back of my mind asks.

Because he swore a blood oath. Because he didn't take Faith. Because he offered to help me get her back.

*Or is it because deep down you still nurture the illusion he's not as rotten as he wants everyone to believe? And because you still have feelings for him,* the voice murmurs.

Does the reason really matter? Just because I didn't

kill him, doesn't mean I trust him. Nobody should ever trust the crown prince of hell. He's a liar, remember? But it's hard to question his selfishness and need for self-preservation. I spent a whole year with him and in all that time he never allowed anyone to cross him. So, yeah, in this particular case, I trust him to be selfish enough to help me find my sister and kill the bastard who took her. Why else would I voluntarily walk into a demon hangout with him and his annoying siblings?

A crooked illuminated cross attached to iron chains hangs on the brick wall. Below it, written in bold black letters, it reads Stairway To Hell. "Classic," I murmur, glaring at the unimaginative name of the bar.

Lev grins. "Don't you like the name?"

"Why not just call it Devil's Bar?" It'd be just as stupid a name as this one.

Verin looks over my shoulder and sighs. "It's an homage."

"To how boring demons are?" I shoot back.

"To one of the greatest bands to ever walk this earth," Lev says, looking like a teenage girl who just came face to face with her idol.

I still don't understand why demons are so crazy about old rock music but whatever. "Led Zeppelin is not the greatest band to ever walk this earth," I say.

"How dare you?" He slams his hand over his heart and acts shocked. "That's blasphemy, you know? You should apologize."

"You'll get over it," I say, half convinced he has a crush on the band.

"I might." Lev inches closer and whispers, "But good old Johny won't appreciate the insult."

"Johny?" I narrow my eyes. "As in John Bonham?"

The drummer of the band died in the eighties as far as I know.

"He's sensitive," Lev says.

"All artists are," Berith adds with a lazy shrug.

It doesn't take much imagination to figure out how Lev knows so much about the dead drummer. In fact, there are only two options: One, the poor dude is part of the prince's exotic collection. Two, he conjured his soul from heaven to make him play his favorite songs. Since both options are pretty messed up, I decide I don't want to know. "Can we get this over with?" I manage a half-smile. "Or do you need a minute alone with Johny to get your obsession out of your system?"

"Let's move," Berith says before Lev can spit his bullshit at me.

The back-alley bar might look like shit from the outside, but on the inside it's pretty fancy. Exquisite marble flooring, chandeliers casting dim but cozy light, black walls decorated with black and white artwork and super comfy looking black velvet sofas—not as shabby as I thought it would be.

"You like it," Lev states.

"I'd like to see it burn," I reply, pushing past him.

The place is crowded. Bodies line the walls. The crowd is mostly demonic. But some unlucky bastards are human, and they have no clue they'll be part of a feast tonight. Pardon, they are the feast.

"I can't believe you." Verin grunts behind us, finally breaking his vow of silence. "You're getting all of us killed."

Lev looks over his shoulder, grinning innocently. "Did anyone ever tell you that you're paranoid?"

"He's not paranoid. He's right and you know it."

Berith sighs. "If the boss finds out you took"—she narrows her eyes at me—"her to one of our joints, he'll come down hard on you."

"On us," Verin grumbles.

"I stand corrected," Berith says. "On us."

"I pissed him off pretty bad, huh?"

Six pairs of eyes find me at once, glaring at me with disbelief. "You slaughtered his best warriors," Lev says. "What do you think?"

"I think he should evaluate his warriors." Taking them down was a piece of cake. So, if they were his best, hell seems to have a real problem.

Verin balls his fists. "Can I just kill her and be done with this shit?" He honors his title as the prince of impatience, and it's obvious he has a hard time keeping his temper in check.

"No!" Lev and I bark in unison.

Berith puts a hand on poor Verin's shoulder. "Patience," she whispers, but her brother continues to sulk like a kid deprived of his favorite teddy bear.

Lev turns to face his grumpy brother. "Nobody is going to lay a finger on her." He winks at me. "Apart from *moi*, of course."

I know they're discussing my end and I guess I should be mad. Maybe under different circumstances, I would be. But as of now, I only care about getting Faith back. When Lev kills me…Well, I can't say I don't deserve punishment for my sins, can I? "Look." I cross my arms, biting my lower lip. "I get that you want me six-feet under, and I promise I won't even put up a fight, but first I need you guys to stop complaining and help me get my sister back, okay?"

Verin's eyes light up. "Does that mean I get to kill

you then?"

"No," comes Lev's sharp reply. "I just told you, no one is touching her except me. Got it?"

"Whatever." Verin grunts. He obviously doesn't like Lev's answer but doesn't argue. "Let's just get this over with."

The second the crowd feels Lev, they stop doing whatever they are doing—dancing, drinking, seducing girls on the dance floor—and part for him.

The idiot enjoys it. He holds his head up high and roams through the packed bar like he owns the fucking world. In a way he does—the underworld, at least.

By the time we reach the bar, all eyes are on us. "What is she doing here?" a blonde demon with an ass that needs two chairs to sit and boobs that go with it whispers.

"Is that...Is that the witch?" her friend asks fearfully.

A tall dude with spiked hair and bad punk-taste nods. "That's the one killing our kind."

"I see you've made friends," Lev says, smiling like an angel.

"Yay me," I reply.

Lev grabs my wrist, pulling me against his side. "Stay close. I wouldn't want to mess up my favorite jeans." Meaning he doesn't want to slaughter the whole bar. Knowing him, it has nothing to do with his jeans and everything to do with the fact they are part of the kingdom he'll eventually inherit. Once daddy dearest retires. *If* daddy dearest retires.

Being so close to him does crazy things to my heart. The bitch in my chest seems to have forgotten about the pain Lev put it through when he told me he had changed his mind about me. I shouldn't have been disappointed. I mean, what did I expect? That the crown prince of hell would give up his crown to be with me? Yeah, unlikely. But when he said those words and when he looked at me like I was more to him than just a witch whose soul he owned, I couldn't help myself. I believed him. Grave mistake. One I don't ever intend to repeat. "I can walk by myself," I mutter.

"Maybe." He winks. "But where's the fun in that?"

I roll my eyes. "What's your father going to say when he hears you cozied up to me in public?"

Lev stops dead in his tracks. "It almost sounds as if you think I'm scared of him."

"Aren't you?" I retort.

Lev sucks his lower lip in, and I can tell he's got plenty to say, but Berith comes to the rescue. "There." She points to a middle-aged dude, rocking salt and pepper hair, sitting all alone on a barstool at the end of the counter. "That's him."

We move toward the guy, my muscles tensing as I feel the demon's energy swirling through the air. "It's been a long time," Lev addresses the demon with a genuine smile.

"Lev?" The demon turns, facing his prince. "Wow! I can't believe it. What brings you to my favorite bar?"

"I was close by and thought I'd pay my old friend a visit."

His gaze darts from Lev to Berith to Verin and eventually rests on me. I swear his eyes almost pop out when he spots me. "And you brought other *friends*?" The dude mutters, "How…Interesting."

Lev pulls me closer, throwing his arm around my shoulder. "Interesting she is." He pauses. "So,

Carnivale, word on the street is someone acquired an earth witch, lately."

"Is that so?" Carnivale plays dumb. "Well, I wouldn't know. Haven't been downstairs in a long time."

"Oh, really?" Lev's laughter chills me to the core. "That's odd. I mean you are the best power-broker in hell, aren't you?"

"I am," Carnivale says proudly. "But not every deal goes through me."

Lev leans against the bar. "Yet, you are aware of every deal made."

Carnivale narrows his eyes at Lev. "What are you saying, *Your Highness*?"

"I'm saying I have a hard time believing a demon like you loses track of his business. Which means one of two things. Either you're getting old and useless, or"—Lev gets in his face—"you're lying to your prince."

The barstool screeches across the wooden floor as the demon jumps to his feet. "Are you questioning my loyalty?"

"I am," Lev replies coldly.

Carnivale's eyes are bright, bloody red, and he looks two seconds from stabbing someone in the neck to feast on their flesh. "That's rich," he spits back. "You know, coming from a guy who defied his father's orders and is clearly consorting with the witch that killed hundreds of us."

Lev might be fuming on the inside, but on the outside, he looks like he just got a massage and is about to head into his next spa session. "Tell me, Carn, how would you know what my father ordered me to do?"

Carnivale's smugness crumbles. "I…I heard about it."

"Did you, now?" Lev leans in. "And who was the little bird spilling his guts?"

Verin obviously has had enough of the false courtesy. Like a damn bulldozer, he pushes past me and grabs Carnivale by the throat. "Tell him!"

"I…I heard whispers."

"Liar," Lev says.

Verin's grip tightens, blocking the airway of Carnivale's vessel and making him squirm. "I swear," he chokes out. "I heard rumors. That's all."

"This is ridiculous," I bark, barely able to hold the fire in my soul under control. "He isn't going to help us."

"Patience," Lev says.

I've been patient and look where it got me—right back to the demon I never wanted to see again, the one for whom I had planned a million painful ways to die. "Don't you remember?" I ask, smiling sweetly as I allow the flames in my soul to take control over my heart, my mind, and my body. "I hate waiting."

"Mel," Lev's warning echoes in my ears as a wave of heat pushes through my palms, setting the counter on fire.

The music stops. Bottles explode. Glass shatters into a million pieces. And then every single demon turns to me, realizing this is just the beginning. "Tell us where Faith is," I demand, flames crawling over every inch of my body.

"Mel," Lev says softly, putting a hand on my shoulder.

"Don't. Touch. Me," I warn, unsure if I can hold

back. He hurt me and the fire within me still demands retribution.

Verin lets go of Carnivale. Then he and Berith step between Lev and me. "Stop it. Now!"

"I don't take orders from you," I retort, allowing a tiny flame to escape my palm, burning Carnivale's cheek.

The bastard screams in agony.

"Where is my sister?" I bark like the crazy witch I am. "Tell me! Tell me, now!"

Lev sighs. "You should listen to her, old friend. When she gets like that no one can stop her."

"Damn, right," I say. No one, not even Lucifer himself can withstand my fire. And as long as no one's putting iron shackles on me, I'm a ticking timebomb.

"All right," Carnivale caves. "I'll tell you."

"Good choice," Lev comments.

I scar his other cheek, too. "Talk!"

Carnivale's gaze turns to Lev. "You have to understand," he argues. "I had little choice but to help him. He has a whole lot of followers, and they are planning your downfall, My Prince."

"Who is he?" I demand, the fire completely out of control. Not just because of Faith, though. No, the fact somebody other than myself is trying to kill Lev messes with my countenance.

Carnivale looks away. "It's Abbadon," he finally whispers. "He took the witch to prove his point."

*Abbadon? No. That can't be.* The demon had once offered me his help. He was sort of nice. You know, for a demon.

**\*\*\*\***

*I gathered my stuff, checked the club one last time*

*to make sure no one hid in the bathroom stalls and finally locked the damn place up. It had been two weeks since Lev had kicked me out and Dana—a fellow witch—had gotten me this job at the club. The pay was miserable, the customers were chauvinistic assholes, and my boss was a rat, but at least it earned me enough to get by and to pay for a shabby motel room, where I lived.*

*Working four fourteen-hour shifts in a row took a toll on me and by the time I stumbled up the stairs of the motel, I felt like I was hit by a truck. The last thing I needed was some weird dude in too tight jeans hitting on me, but the guy didn't seem to care about my resting bitch-face. He walked right up to me and said, "A princess like you shouldn't be out here by herself in the middle of the night."*

*"And a guy like you," I retorted. "Should know better than to hit on a girl like me in the middle of the night."*

*He laughed. "Ah, Melissani. I can see why my prince was so smitten with you."*

*Fear rolled down my spine. "Who are you?" Did Lev change his mind? Did he send one of his goons to collect my soul ahead of time? Did he—*

*"Let me introduce myself," he said, bowing low and grabbing my hand to plant a kiss on my knuckles. "My name is Abbadon, I am a great duke of hell and I'm here to make you an offer."*

*I pulled my hand back and glared at him. "I'm done making deals with hell's royalty." The last one hadn't just cost me my soul but my heart, too.*

*He stepped back, giving me some much-needed space. "I understand. I do." He cocked his head to the* side and studied me. "From what I've gathered our prince didn't treat you well."

"What do you want?" I barked, not in the mood to talk about Lev.

"The question is what do you want, Melissani?"

"What's that supposed to mean?"

He drew a deep breath. "You and my prince didn't part on the best of terms, did you?"

I crossed my arms. "And what's that to you?"

He shrugged. "See, I know he can be a little...Difficult."

"Difficult?" I couldn't help but laugh. "That's an interesting description." I would have chosen the words asshole, idiot, obnoxious rat...But difficult would do the trick, too.

Abbadon's lips curled into an honest smile. "I assume you wouldn't want to spend the rest of eternity serving him, would you?"

"Do I have a choice?"

"Yes," came his reply. "You actually do."

I should have told him to bugger off. Instead, I said, "I'm listening."

He nodded. "I can solve your problem. All you have to do is convince the prince to trade your soul for another."

"And why would he do that?" I was a hellfire witch and Lev knew how powerful I was. "He'd never give up that kind of power."

He arched a brow. "Why don't we give it a try? Nor harm, no foul."

I should have walked away, should have burned the demon, but the thought of an eternity with Lev was so much worse than any other fate. "And how am I *supposed to find him?"*

*"He's currently in DC." The demon rattled off an address and then he was gone, vanished into thin air.*

\*\*\*\*

"Abbadon?" Berith shrill voice brings me back. "That's impossible."

Lev doesn't seem to share his sister's sentiment. He narrows his eyes at Carnivale. "And what point would that be?"

"That you…" He swallows hard. "That the love you feel for the witch weakens you."

"Love?" God, I haven't laughed this hard in years. "Are you insane? The dude doesn't even know what that is." Well, except for self-love maybe, that he knows plenty about.

"You're wrong," Carnivale says. "He—"

He drops to the floor, a gaping hole in his chest, while Lev holds his heart, grinning at the onlookers. "Would anybody else like to test my strength?"

The demons scatter, running like chickens.

"Is that a no?" Lev yells after them, grinning like a lunatic holding a damn heart in his palm.

"That's a no," Berith assures him.

"Good." He drops the heart. "Then, let's go and have a little chat with my man Abbadon."

I should tell Lev about the offer, should let him know it was Abbadon who offered to trade my soul for another. But the fire in my palm roars like a lion, clearly saying it's not in a chatty mood.

"Mel?" Green eyes study me.

"What?" I hiss.

He nods at my burning body. "Somebody is going to call the news, if you walk out of here like a human torch."

He has a point. It's just...Pulling the fire back has never been harder. I swear, all I want is to burn the whole joint down.

"Think about your sister," he whispers.

He's right. I can always come back after we free her. And when I do, none of these bitches will come out alive.

## Chapter 19

*Leviathan*

We are headed to the top-secret location of one of hell's hidden portals. Yes, I'm being sly on purpose. I wouldn't want some stupid humans—no offense—to conduct a demon hunt, using their pointless EMF-readers and all that other nonsense you see on TV nowadays. Can you imagine what would happen if a couple of teenagers found the place and brought a Ouija board along? Sorry, but I refuse to be conjured by some wannabees to cure their acne. That's where I draw the line. Anyway, so we're headed to the portal and the night sky is lit by millions of stars, shining down on us like happy angel campers. I swear, it's almost as if heaven enjoys this shit-show, winking down on us from above, hoping our mission ends in death.

*Death* the word roars through my brain, reminding me of what I should be concerned about—the tiny fact some of my own kind are plotting my downfall, trying to take away what I acquired with lots of blood and sweat. But my concerns rest with Mel instead. Once again, the witch has infiltrated my every thought and now I can only think of her. Of the way the greenish flames of hellfire licked over her smooth skin, the fierce look in her eyes when she burned Carn's cheek—sweet baby Satan, she was hot. So hot, I wanted to push her petite frame against the bar, taking her right then and there while everyone watched. Screwing her like I used to. You know, before I tossed her fine butt out of my bed and told her we never had a future, that it was all just a sweet illusion. It was true back then. When we started our little affair, Mel's soul was still pure. The little witch had no idea what she was getting herself into when she climbed into my bed. At the beginning, I didn't mind ruining her. I reveled in the idea of making her every bit as tainted as I'd known she'd become if she spent more time with me. But...Things changed. I changed. And when I spoke to Verin about leaving hell behind and my brother accused her of hexing me, I...Well, I believed him. Old me would have never given up the chance to sit on the throne, so I figured Verin was right. Mel must have used her magic to mess with my brain, which meant I had already successfully ruined her. And somehow, I just couldn't live with the thought of corrupting her anymore. The witch was eventually going to be mine, I figured I'd allow her a couple of good years, doing all the silly things girls dreamed of, before I added her soul to my collection of rotten creatures. I never considered the possibility she might end up ruining herself. But Mel always had the tendency to make wrong choices. How else did she end up falling in love with the crown prince of hell? Me, the very demon who bought her soul from her own mother, because I have a thing for exotic stuff like the soul of a hellfire witch (or the drummer of my favorite band).

"You're awfully quiet," Mel says, as we reach our destination. "Are you afraid of Abbadon or what?"

I snicker. "Or what, love." Sure, the duke is powerful and the fact my father cherishes him and his advice isn't making things easier—those two have been pretty close ever since they fell together—but he's not half as cunning and smart as I am.

"Don't underestimate him," Berith warns. "He's powerful and if Carnivale was right, he isn't alone."

Verin rolls his eyes. "Neither is Lev."

Berith frowns. "Three demons and a wacky witch? Those aren't exactly great odds."

"One crown prince, a princess, a prince and a hellfire witch," I correct her. "Call me crazy, but I'd say those are fantastic odds." (I have won wars with far less skilled warriors.)

"I still don't get it." Mel's gaze darts to me. "Why would Abbadon abduct Faith?"

"To play you," Verin answers with an eye-roll that would make any Hollywood diva jealous.

Mel shakes her head. "That doesn't make any sense."

"Why not?" Berith asks.

Mel sighs. "Because…" She kicks a stone and won't look up.

"What's the matter, Mel?"

"Remember the demon who offered to trade my soul for another?"

"What about him?" I ask, not keen on where this conversation is headed.

For a long time, she stands there quietly glaring at her sneakers. Then, eventually she says, "It was Abbadon. He offered to make the trade."

"He what?" I bark.

My sister eyes Mel curiously. "Abbadon approached you to get Lev to trade your soul for another?"

Mel nods.

*I'm going to kill the bastard! No, I won't kill him. I'll skin him alive, and I'll take my sweet time doing it.*

Verin studies both Mel and me. "I don't get it," he admits eventually. "Why would Abbadon think you would give up the soul of a hellfire witch for another?"

The beast in my chest rages and the last thing I want is to anger it further. I fear it might slaughter anyone in the vicinity if that were to happen. So, I draw several deep breaths and reply, "Because he owns a soul I've been wanting for a very long time."

"Who's soul?" Verin pushes.

I could order him to shut up, could simply change the topic or threaten his manhood if he ever dared to ask again, but something tells me my siblings wouldn't cave this time. They want answers and since they're about to go against our father just to help me, I owe them. "Alina's soul."

"Alina?" Berith's eyes go wide. "*The* Alina?"

I shrug. "Do you know any other Alina?"

"Who is Alina?" Mel asks confused.

"She's…"

"His mother," Verin says because he knows I can't get the word out of my mouth.

"Wait!" Mel stops. "Abbadon has the soul of your mother?" I shrug it off as if it weren't a big thing. (And it isn't. Alina was my mother in another life. When I was still human and pathetic. Now, I'm the crown prince of hell and attachments aren't my thing.) "And he offered to trade it for mine?"

"Looks like it." I force a smile. "But I had no idea he was the demon who sent you that night."

Mel blinks several times. "A-and…I-if y-you had known?" she stammers. "What if I had mentioned his name?" She sounds as if she feels terribly guilty for neglecting to share the bastard's name.

She doesn't need to be. "My answer would have been the same." No, I am not trying to be charming or romantic or whatever it is you think…I'm just honest and while I do want my human mother's soul, I would never give up Mel's. She's too powerful.

She glares at me. "B-but—" She shakes her head. "How is that even possible? How can he possess your mother's soul?"

I'm so not in the mood to talk family, but Mel won't leave me be unless I give her something. So, I go with my favorite half-truth. "My mother was human, and she struck a deal with Abbadon. It was her choice. End of the story."

Mel stares at me as if I've grown angel wings. "You…I…I don't even know what to say to that."

"Nothing," I say. "Now, let's move. We need the element of surprise." And I hope none of the surviving demons from the club spilled the news already.

We reach the stone mausoleum and Mel suddenly grabs my wrist. Her touch sends electric jolts through my chest. "Listen," she says, her gaze darting from the final resting place of some poor bastard to me. "You don't have to come with me. I can do this on my own."

"Sounds like a lot of fun," I reply. "But I wouldn't want to miss this party, love." I turn to my impatient siblings. "Prepare the portal, will ya?"

They nod and disappear inside the grave, working on the ritual that will take us through the portal and straight to Abbadon.

Mel and I wait outside, making sure no unwanted visitors interrupt the two. Humans have the tendency to roam around places they shouldn't. And we can't have them finding the portal. Even hell has to stick to the rules and making sure our world is hidden from the humans is a major one.

"I meant it," she says after some time. "You don't have to help me. I can take care of this demon myself."

"No, you can't," I assure her.

A spark of fire flashes across her eyes. "Don't make the mistake of underestimating me, Lev. I'm not the witch I used to be."

"Oh, really? Well, I couldn't tell." She's anything but the witch that used to make me pancakes and forced me to watch stupid shows. This version of Mel is darker and a lot sexier. Not that she wasn't hot before, but there's something about a girl who embraces her darkness. And that something drives me a little wild.

Mel eyes me suspiciously. "Your father is going to fuck you up really badly if you help me."

"He's going to"—I draw quotation marks in the air— "fuck me up really badly just because you're still breathing," I admit. "Yet, here you are, alive and well."

Her gaze darts to the crescent moon, lingering above us like a scythe that's two seconds away from severing our heads from our torsos. "I won't put up a fight."

"Come again?"

She blows out a long breath. "Once we free Faith, and you follow through with your dad's orders, I won't put up a fight."

"Why, are you suicidal or something?" I retort, keeping my face straight and the odd feeling in my gut at bay.

"No." Mel smiles, but it never reaches her eyes.

"I'm just tired, Lev. That's all."

"Tired of living?" I glare at her. "That's sort of the same as suicidal, you know?" I mean, the Germans don't call suicidal folks *lebensmüde* (life-tired) for no reason.

The witch with the breathtaking green eyes leans against the wall of the mausoleum and shrugs. "There are worse things than death."

"Like your soul ending up in hell? Like you becoming my slave, bound to do my bidding?" Because that's exactly what'll happen if I kill her. Her soul will be reaped by death and returned to me to use whenever I need her.

Mel sighs. "Hell isn't just a place, Lev."

"What are you saying, Melissani?" She sounds like the Oracle of Delphi when she predicted the downfall of Leonidas. And as previously mentioned I'm not a fan of the envious old hag.

Her expression is void of emotion as she pushes herself off the wall to face me. "I'm saying I'm counting on you to fulfill your father's wish when we find Faith."

Is she asking me to kill her? "Why?"

"Why not?" she replies. "We both know I was never meant to be born in the first place. So, you'd simply be correcting nature's mistake."

She's lost it. She's officially crossed the borders of mad-world. "What in Satan's name happened to you, Mel?" And why does my chest constrict at the thought of ending her?

A sad smile tugs at the corner of her mouth. "Life, Lev. Life happened to me."

I never get the chance to reply, because Berith

walks out of the crypt and announces, "We're ready."

## Chapter 20

*Melissani*

Berith and Verin don't disappoint. By the time Lev and I join them in the mausoleum, the portal—a gaping black hole—is already staring back at us. The odd scene should probably freak me out. There is a black tunnel leading straight to hell in the wall of the mausoleum, but a million thoughts race through my mind and one is louder and more demanding than any other. *He offered the soul of Lev's mother in exchange for mine and he...wouldn't make the deal.*

Why?

Yes, Leviathan is a demon. He's ruthless and without a conscience. Well, at the very least, he acts that way. I used to believe it was a façade. Now, I'm not so sure about that anymore. That's beside the point though. Because I know for a fact Lev cared about his mother.

\*\*\*\*

*"Is that Piper Halliwell's voice again?" Lev asked.*

*I jammed the phone between my ear and my shoulder and rose to switch off the TV. "Nope."*

*"Liar," he laughed.*

*I rolled my eyes. "What's a girl have to do besides watching reruns?" Lev was somewhere in Europe, doing business with some politician, and I was bored out of my mind.*

136

*"You are aware there's more to life than watching TV, aren't you?" he teased me, but something else tinged in his voice. I thought it sounded like concern, but I knew Lev well enough to delete the idea quickly from my brain's desktop. He was a demon and despite the fact he wasn't what I had expected the crown prince of hell to be, I couldn't allow myself to forget who I was dealing with. It bore the risk of losing more than just my soul and chastity and that was too dangerous.*

*I diverted the topic. "When will you be back?"*

*"Tomorrow," he said. "Things are going well."*

*I wasn't sure I liked that. "So, you managed to corrupt another politician, and bring about World War III?" I laughed, but it was only half a joke.*

*"He was already corrupted by his greed and may I remind you, I'm not one of the four horsemen. Also, war isn't really my thing. It bores me."*

*"Then what is your thing?"*

*"You," he replied, voice husky. "You're my thing."*

*It was so easy to buy his lies and for now, I just couldn't bring myself to dig for the truth. "So, what does Your Royal Highness suggest I do with my spare time?"*

*"Have some fun?" he said and quickly added. "Not the kind of fun we have, because I'm not the sharing type, but you know...Dress up, go out, hang with your little witch friend. That sort of stuff."*

*That wasn't such a bad idea. "I haven't seen Dana in ages."*

*"Go then." He sighed. "I'll see you tomorrow."*

*"Don't destroy Europe," I warned him. "There are still places I haven't seen yet."*

*"I'll do my best," he promised and hung up.*

*Motivated, I headed straight for the bedroom to get some clothes. They were stored in Lev's closet and when I opened the door, I caught side of a little wooden box I had never before seen. I knew I should have left it alone, shouldn't have opened it, but my fingers were quicker than my brain and by the time I realized how wrong it was to snoop in his private belongings, it was already too late.*

*Inside the box was a lock of black hair tied together with a blue ribbon. It looked like a curl from a child and reminded me of an old tradition where parents kept some hair from their newborns as a memory. I always thought it a weird tradition, especially considering what someone like me—a witch—could do with a strand of hair. But whatever. Next to the lock was a small drawing. It was that of a woman, looking like one of those Greek goddesses with her baby boy sitting on her lap. I can't say why I felt the urge to take the drawing out of the box, but when I turned it over, I found an inscription. It said, "To my little Leviathan. I will always love you. Mama."*

*I couldn't quite comprehend what I'd just read. Lev had a mother? He was a demon. How—*

*Stupid question. Of course, I knew how babies were made. Apparently, baby demons were conceived the same way. Which made sense because I too was half demon. Yet the fact Lev had a mother, and he kept this drawing made me…It made me wonder if maybe he did have a heart after all. Why else would he have kept those things?*

****

I shake the memory off and pay little attention to Lev, who ogles me like I'm growing fangs and fairy-wings at the same time and move closer to the dark hole in the stone wall. The energy signature erupting from the portal jolts through my veins, waking the fire inside me. "All right," I say, rubbing my sweaty palms across my jeans. "Shall we?"

"This is a bad idea." Berith snorts as Lev steps into the portal, holding out his hand for me.

For a second, I consider smacking it, but then I realize I have no idea how portals work or what's waiting for us inside and grab his hand.

"Hold on tight, love," are the last words Lev utters, before the darkness swallows us, pulling us deeper and deeper into a world made of pain and sorrow.

I have no clue how long the journey takes. It feels like forever and just a few seconds at the same time, but when the hole spits us out, tossing us onto a black marble floor, I find myself in awe. I mean, who knew hell had such pretty flooring, right?

"You good?" Lev asks, pulling me to my feet.

I shake his hand off. "Perfect."

Verin's gaze darts between the two of us, then he shakes his head and says, "We are so fucked."

"More than fucked," Berith adds.

Lev waves the two off. "Let's just find Abbadon, okay?"

It's not often I find myself agreeing with the prick, but in this case, I have little choice. "Lead the way."

Chapter 21

*Melissani*

Hell is not what I expected. I have had plenty of time to consider my future home. In my mind, I saw fire and brimstone, dead plants and dried earth and monsters lurking in every corner. But this…It looks like a fancy five-star hotel and not just because of the expensive marble floor. "This is hell?" I hear myself blurt.

Lev turns to face me, a glimpse of amusement flickering over his lips. "What did you expect?"

"Fire and brimstone," Verin mutters. "What else?"

Lev eyes me. "You did, didn't you?"

I shrug. "Who doesn't?"

"Ignorance," Berith grumbles. "Such a pitiful human trait."

"I'm not human," I remind her.

"No," she agrees. "But you're obviously not immune to their prejudices."

"Prejudices?" I laugh. "We're talking about hell. What does one expect? Fields of daisies and daffodils?"

"Not here," Lev says. "They only grow in the Limbo."

"Seriously?" He can't mean that. Can he?

"You should see Berith's garden," Lev says. "It puts the Queen of England's to shame." A demon princess who likes gardening? Goddess, I might need a drink to get through this without losing my damn mind.

I drink in the fancy—for lack of a better description—hotel lobby and I'm thoroughly confused. "In all seriousness, this looks like any five-star hotel."

"Because it is a five-star hotel," Verin murmurs, rolling his eyes.

"Hell is a five-star hotel?" And here I thought, I'd have to spend the rest of eternity sleeping on a rock.

"A five-star hotel in Rome," Berith adds with a smirk. She obviously enjoys this.

I on the other hand…Well, I'm still confused. "Okay, can someone fill me in? Why is hell a five-star hotel in Rome?"

Lev blows out a frustrated breath. "Hell is so much more than this, Mel."

"Explain," I order.

"It's a long story," he assures me.

"Make it a short one," I demand.

"Fine." He shoves his hands in his pockets and says, "See, most people believe hell is a single place. They think it's hidden down below."

"I look around, taking in our surroundings. "But it isn't?"

He shakes his head. "No. Hell, is pretty much an extension of earth."

"Wait." I slam my hands on my hips. "So, when demons are sent back to hell, they're really just sent back here?" I gesture at the walls.

"You're getting it all wrong," Verin mutters.

"Then help me get it straight!" I will spend the rest of forever here. It's the fair thing to do.

Berith steps forward. "Lev is right. It is a long and complicated story, but in short, hell is on earth, but it's based in another dimension."

"Like the *Twilight Zone*?"

"Sort of," Lev says.

"This is so wrong." I mean, all this time people feared fire and brimstone when in reality they were literally walking through hell on a daily basis, because it exists in a parallel dimension right next to them.

"It is what it is," Lev says,

"Yeah, and if you're done with the Q&A session, I suggest we get going." Verin studies our surroundings. "Unless you would like to see why, despite my sister's green thumb, hell isn't for the faint of heart."

"He's right." Lev sighs. "Let's not keep our old friend waiting."

Lev guides us down a narrow hallway. Breathtaking artwork decorates the walls. The paintings look like they belong in the Louvre, not some parallel hell dimension. We move down the dimly lit hallway, and I continue to be awestruck by the beauty of it all. There's lots of black and plenty of red, but the black is the finest marble and the most intriguing chandeliers, and the red belongs to soft velvet curtains, covering the entrances of rooms.

We make it to the end of the hallway when the sound of footsteps echoes off the walls. "Shit," Lev hisses.

Fear wraps its needy hand around my throat. "What is it?"

Lev ignores my question and turns to Verin. "I thought she was out and about."

Verin sighs. "What can I say? She's unpredictable like that."

"Who is she?" I ask, a little worried about their

142

reaction to what's coming toward us.

"Amazing," Lev grumbles once again ignoring me. "Now what?"

Berith crosses her arms above her chest. "She won't be pleased to see"—she nods at me—"her."

"You don't say." Lev shakes his head. "We've got about two seconds before she gets here. So, any bright ideas?"

"Who—"

"We'll distract her," Berith cuts me off. "Hide her."

From whom? I want to ask, confused about them acting like they aren't the princes and princess of hell. I never get the chance though. Lev grabs me by the arm and pulls me through one of the curtains, while Berith and Verin stay behind.

"What the fuck?" I snort.

He pushes me against the wall, covering my mouth with his hand. "Shh."

I consider biting the prick, but before I get the chance to do so, my gaze drifts over his shoulder to a set of sofas. Or should I say to the four couples, exchanging bodily fluids on said sofas.

One look at my face and Lev laughs. "Welcome to the first circle," he whispers as the four enjoy each other. Wait, why do these people look so familiar. Aren't they—

"Not a sound," Lev whispers in my ear, pushing harder against me than he has to. "If she finds you here, she'll alert my father and that wouldn't be a meeting you'd like to attend. Do you hear me, love?" His green eyes pierce mine and when I nod, he slowly takes his hand off my mouth. "Just stay still." He adds as if I needed another warning.

Outside the footsteps grow louder. Sounds like high heels clicking against the marble floor. A moment later, I hear the low voice of a woman, a voice that penetrates my brain and makes me feel like I'm floating on clouds. "Prince Verin and Princess Berith, to what do I owe the pleasure?"

"We're on our way to see the duke," Berith replies sweetly. "But tell me, Helen, how've you been? It's been ages."

My brain starts to connect the dots. We are in the circle of lust and that woman is called Helen? "Please tell me we aren't hiding from Helen of Troy."

"We are," Lev confirms.

"Why?" I shake my head. "Since when are you scared of a human?"

"She's not human anymore," Lev explains.

I narrow my eyes. "Then what is she?"

"A succubus."

I almost burst into laughter. "Helen of Troy is a succubus? Why? How?" And why does that even surprise me? She was known for her seductive skills in life, so it shouldn't surprise me that she upped her game a notch in death.

Lev looks over his shoulder to the quartet on the sofa. Their moans fill the room, making the air thick with the scent of pleasure and joy. "Hell changes everyone."

"Did it change you?" I ask.

He drew closer, his lips brushing over the tender skin on my neck. "What do you think?"

What do I think? I honestly don't know. The longer I'm in here, the harder it is to make sense of my thoughts. It's as if something messes with my senses, turning everything into a foggy chaos. Well, everything except...

Lev's lips.

Lev's closeness.

Lev's hot breath.

And...

The scene on the sofa. My gaze is glued to the familiar couples and while my heart doesn't quite know what to make of that scene, my libido...Well, let's just say, there's a good chance I'll be joining the bunch once Lev kills me.

"I always figured you'd like watching," Lev whispers, giving me a taste of the growing beast inside his pants. "But while watching is fun"—his hand wanders down my belly and into my waistband—"doing it is so much better, don't you think?"

The instant his long fingers run over my panties I stiffen. It has nothing to do with him invading my most private space and everything to do with the fact I love it to the point where I can't withhold the moan of pleasure working its way up my throat. "Stop," I hiss through his fingers.

In a heartbeat, Lev pulls his hand out of my pants and smirks. "Your wish is my command, love."

"Since when?" I hear myself ask, while a bunch of curses sit on the tip of my tongue, waiting for me to let them escape.

Lev eyes the couples, still entangled in each other, not giving a shit that they have witnesses. "Since we're in the circle of lust."

"You are making no sense," I mutter, pushing the fire in my loins to the darkest part of my soul. The box labeled Dangerous as Fuck.

"I'm making perfect sense," he says, letting go of my hand and finally giving me some space to breathe in air instead of his intoxicating scent. "Every emotion, especially the naughty ones, are heightened down here."

"So?"

He grins, moving incredibly close to my mouth. "So, here's the deal. Next time I'm inside you, I want you to scream my name because you can't help it. Not because your uncontrolled lust jumbles with your hormones."

"Next time?" I laugh. "There'll be no next time."

"Guess we'll just have to wait and see about that, won't we?"

"Lev?" Verin barks outside the swinger-club room. "Come out. She's gone."

## Chapter 22

*Leviathan*

I do my best to forget all about our little excursion to the first circle and the way Mel's body reacted to me, like we were old friends, and it welcomed my intrusion despite everything that had happened. Right now, I need to keep my head in the game, because we are about to walk into Abbadon's playground. The Duke of Destruction owns the Italian territory and resides in…Well, in a famous landmark protected by his goons also known as Scavengers—once human, the creatures are now nothing but vultures, feeding on the remains of…Just about anything.

"Wait," Verin says as we turn onto Porta Sant' Anna. "Maybe we should come up with a plan or something?"

"I have a plan," I assure him.

"Which is?" Mel asks.

"Simple," I say. "Walk in, get your sister, kill the idiot, and get out."

Berith sighs. "You can't just kill him. He's a damn duke."

"And I'm the crown prince," I shoot back. "Last time I checked, crown prince trumped duke, doesn't it?"

"Yeah, it does," Berith says. "But you know damn well his death will lead to a civil war. Other demons will try to take his spot, to rule over his legions."

"Let them," I say, coolly. "We'll deal with them when the time comes."

Mel stares at me. "Maybe you should listen to your sister," she suggests. "I can do this on my own."

"You can." She's strong enough to take down Abbadon and his treacherous friends, no doubt about it. "But you won't." This is as much my battle as it is hers and I'll be damned if I let the bastard get away with his dirty game. He's been breathing down my neck for far too long and if it hadn't been for my father, I would have long ended his pitiful existence. At least now I have a good reason. One my father can't argue about.

Not waiting them to come up with more reasons as to why this is a stupid idea, I head down the old street and walk right up to—

"Is that…" Mel shakes her head at the scene. "No, it can't be, right?"

"The Vatican City," I assure her. "Or hell's version of it." The city rises high into the black sky, but the famous landmark looks like Pearl Harbor after the attack of the Japanese. Smoke rises into the night sky and the walls of the prestigious buildings are swallowed by an ocean of flames. I like chaos as much as any demon, but that sort of destruction and ugliness isn't my cup of tea. I prefer tidy chaos if you know what I mean.

"I…I don't know what to say." Mel draws a deep breath. "So, I'm just going to ignore the reality that Vatican City is part of hell and move on to how we find Abbadon."

I point to the burning city. "He's right there."

"Inside the Vatican?" she asks, clearly unable to

comprehend the concept of hell. I can't blame her. It took me ages to wrap my head around it.

"Inside hell's Vatican," Berith corrects her.

"Demons," Mel mutters. "You guys are so messed up."

"Says the witch who set a poor, helpless old woman on fire," Verin shoots back.

"Georgina was not helpless," Mel say, but I taste her regret as much as I taste my own need, awakened by that stupid excursion to the circle of lust.

Verin flashes her a devilish grin. "Semantics."

"You—"

"Come on." I grab her arm and pull her through the entrance. "You can insult my brother after we save your sister."

Within a few moments, we reach Saint Peter's Square. Mel stops dead in her tracks, taking everything in. Her gaze darts from the bloody waters of the Fontana del Bernini to the inverted wooden crosses lined up on each side of the square. Human remains are scattered on the ground. Souls scream in pure agony. "What the actual fuck?"

"Ignore them," I order, tugging her along.

"But those souls—"

"Get what they deserve," Berith assures her. "Everyone does in hell."

"There." I point ahead at Abbadon's mansion, otherwise known as St. Peter's Basilica or the world's largest basilica of Christianity.

"This is so fucked-up," Mel whispers.

"Get a grip," Berith orders. "We've got bigger fish to fry." She sighs. "Like them."

Mel follows Berith's gaze and she instinctively

steps back, stumbling right into me. "Easy," I say.

"Wh-what the hell are those?" she stammers, never taking her eyes off the deformed ex-humans, crawling toward us.

I ignore their unhinged jaws, their yellowish shark-like teeth, and the stink they bring with them and say, "Scavengers." And a whole lot of them, too. "They're nasty buggers who would be thrilled to devour a pretty thing like you."

Mel glares at me. "If I didn't know better, I'd say you're concerned about my well-being, Your Evil Highness."

I narrow my eyes at her. "You should know better."

"What now?" Mel asks, obviously disturbed by the creatures.

"Kill them," Verin barks.

"And try not to get bitten," I add.

Berith nods. "Their bites are venomous."

"Like snakes?"

"Worse," I say as I take a deep breath and free the beast inside me.

It only takes a heartbeat for the darkness to take over. It slams against my ribcage, hammers against my brain, and slowly conquers every fiber of my being. The power-surge is intoxicating, taking me to a high that makes me feel like I can fly. I let it flood my system, allow it to take the wheel and once it settles into the driver seat, I sit back and watch from the sidelines as my darkness pushes through my palms, finding its first victims.

Scavengers are a lot like Zombies, brainless and dumb. So, it doesn't surprise me when they keep slithering toward us, even though my darkness has already wrapped itself around the necks of at least twenty of their friends, choking the death out of them.

Verin and Berith prefer hands on combat. I watch them from the corner of my eyes as they slice throat after throat, offing them by the dozen.

Of course, Mel doesn't just stand by. She fries the creatures, tossing her green flames at their already withering corpses, turning them to ash and dust.

"They keep coming," Verin yells as my darkness finds its newest victims, offing them quicker than the ones before.

Berith shoves her blade through the skull of a Scavenger and sighs. "He's right." She looks ahead. "We can't kill them all."

"You're wrong," I assure her.

"Fine," my sister hisses. "We can but by the time we're done with them, Abbadon will know we're here."

She's right. "So, how about Plan B."

"There's a plan B?" Mel asks, shaking one of the filthy creatures off her leg, seconds before it can slam its rotten teeth into her skin.

I flash her a smile. "Remember the castle?"

Berith and Verin freeze. "I sure hope you're not referencing the castle she blew up last week."

"I am," I say, coolly. Then I turn to Mel. "Word on the street is that you took down the whole place with a single flame."

"I…It…" She draws a deep breath. "I was angry."

I nod at the creatures. "So, be angry."

Another Scavenger grabs her leg, trying to sink its teeth into her. She burns its face off, eyeing me confused. "It doesn't work like that, Lev. I can't just be angry."

"You can't?" I roll my eyes. "Fine, then be a coward. Stand here and wait till Abbadon, the demon you wanted to give your soul to, kills your beloved little sister."

"Shut up," she yells, her eyes greener than ever before.

"Why?" I goad her. "It's true, isn't it? You are responsible for all of this and no matter how much you hate to admit it, you know I'm right."

Sparks lick over her arms and cheeks. "I said, shut up, Lev."

"Dude." Verin is next to me. "Do you really think it's a good idea to mess with her when she's like that?"

I pay him no attention and step closer to Mel, smashing a Scavengers head with my boots in the process. "Do you know why it was so easy for you to believe I was responsible for Faith's fate?" I ask, my lips brushing her earlobe as her body tenses. "You needed a scapegoat, Mel. Needed someone to blame for your own mistakes." I point at the creatures. "Look at them. Your sister might as well be dead. And it's your fault."

"Shut up!" she screams as a heatwave erupts from her. It's so strong it pushes me ten feet backward.

Verin shouts something, but his voice is drowned out by a tornado of flames, swirling over the remaining Scavengers and burning them alive.

The show—a very impressive show, I might add— is over in less than a minute and when the last Scavenger turns to dust, Mel's fire turns into a cloud of green smoke and she drops to her knees, blood streaming from her nose.

I get to my feet, reaching her in a heartbeat. "Are you okay?"

She looks up from underneath hooded lashes, the anger still brewing in her beautiful eyes. "I hate you. I fucking hate you, Leviathan."

"I know," I reply, even though I taste something very different on the tip of my tongue. "I know." I grab her arm, slowly helping her to her feet.

She leans against my chest, her body trembling with exhaustion when Verin and Berith finally dare to come closer. "I can see why our father dreads your existence," Berith says and while it should sound offensive, but it actually sounds like a compliment.

Verin bites his lower lip. "Remind me not to piss you off again, okay?"

"Will do," Mel replies, grinning at my brother. "But I doubt it would hold you back." She's right. Verin isn't the kind of guy who thinks things through. He acts first, thinks…Well, never.

Berith looks ahead at the walls of the basilica. "We better get going. Pretty sure Abbadon felt her power."

Every demon in hell did. Even my father and that…Well, it concerns me. "Yeah, let's go get this over with." Preferably before my father joins the fun.

Chapter 23

*Melissani*

We move past the ashes of the Scavengers toward the famous basilica, which serves as the backbone of Catholicism. The walls of the church are smeared with what looks like fresh blood. "That's so gross."

"He's always been a bit morbid," Lev says.

"Morbid, huh?" That's one way of describing Abbadon's sick taste. Between the blood-spouting fountain, those Scavengers and the bloody walls of a church, I'd say we crossed the line of morbid already. "That's not morbid. It's—"

"Hell," Verin cuts in. "What did you expect? Beds of roses?"

"No," I say. "Surely not that."

"Come on, guys!" Berith is already halfway past the burned remains of the Scavengers. "We're on the clock, remember?"

She's right and I swear, I try to move faster, but my stupid feet are…Well, I'm not at my best. Allowing the fire to take over took a toll on me.

"Go on," Lev says, suddenly beside me. "We're right behind you." He wraps his arm around my hip, steadying me. "Are you sure you can do this?" He eyes me skeptically. "You can sit this one out. I will get Faith back to you."

"No." I shake my head and force my spine straight.

"She's my sister and I won't just chill the hell out, while you…" What? Save her? Since when is Lev the shining knight in armor? He isn't. "Why are you doing this?" I ask him, as I allow him to guide me toward his siblings.

"I have no idea what you're talking about," he replies, keeping his gaze on the path ahead.

I clear my throat and swallow my pride. "Why are you helping me? I wanted to kill you, remember?"

"So?" He shrugs. "You wanted to kill me, and I bought your soul. I'd say we're even."

"Are we?" I shake my head. "I slaughtered your friends, Lev." A bitter taste crawls up my gullet. "I would have slaughtered your siblings, too."

"I'm aware," he says nonchalantly.

"Then why help me?" I push.

He grins. "Who says I'm helping you?" He looks up at the smoky sky. "I've always hated Abbadon, and he wants my head, remember?"

"I do," I say. "But that doesn't mean you need to free Faith. You could kill him and…" I trail off, unable to say the words.

"And what?"

I shrug. "And keep my sister's soul as a trophy."

He laughs wholeheartedly. "Sorry, Mel. But one of you is more than enough." He meets my gaze. "I don't think anyone could deal with the two of you at the same time."

I nudge him. "We're not that bad."

"Oh, yes. Yes, you are." Eerie silence falls between us, then he stops dead in his tracks and puts two fingers under my chin, making me look him in the eye. "This changes nothing, though." He pauses. "Sure, we were played and hopefully, my father will rethink your death, but if he orders me to kill you, I won't have a choice."

"I know." I draw a deep breath. "I didn't expect anything less from the crown prince of hell." And I'm not nearly dumb enough to believe I'll make it out of here alive. That's okay, though. All I care about is Faith.

"Guys!" Berith waves impatiently. "Can you hurry?"

We can and we do.

## Chapter 24

*Leviathan*

We've barely crossed the threshold of St. Peter's Basilica, when real hell hits us right in the face. My sister's jaw drops. "What the actual fuck?"

"Is this for real?" Verin says, eyes wide open.

Mel just glares at the scene unfolding before our very eyes and then...She laughs. "This...This is...Wow. Just wow."

I wouldn't exactly use the word "wow" to describe the scenario and although I'm no fan of the f-word my sister seems to love so much, it's the best way to describe this madness. Right inside St. Peter's Basilica is a massive pool and inside said pool, lies Abbadon, the Duke of Destruction, on an inflated unicorn, wearing matching unicorn sunglasses. "Lev," he says the second he spots us. "What brings you to my humble kingdom?"

"More like humble unicorn slash plush kitten hell," Mel says, taking in the endless collection of all-things unicorn and kittens.

The demon paddles to the edge of the pool, grabs a unicorn towel to cover his puny manhood (no wonder the ladies give him a wide berth) and gets out of the water. "And look at that." His head jerks in Mel's direction. "You brought me a gift." He takes his stupid sunglasses off and flashes her a wicked smile that reeks of pure evil. "Hello, dear Melissani, the infamous witch wreaking havoc. It's been too long, hasn't it? Tell me, my dear, how've you been?"

Mel isn't nearly as stunned about the unicorn disaster as the rest of us and gets right down to business. "Where is my sister?"

Abbadon smiles like an angel who hasn't fallen from grace. "Oh, you mean lovely Faith?"

Hellfire roars in Mel's eyes and I know she's seconds from blowing us all into bits and pieces. "Where is she?"

"Right here," Abbadon says, pointing to an eight-foot high, wooden unicorn standing next to the pool. "Inside the belly of my Trojan horse."

"Trojan horse?" Verin laughs. "It's a damn unicorn, Abb."

He shrugs Verin's comment off. "Sometimes the history books get it wrong." He moves toward the wooden monstrosity and pats its belly. "This beauty caused a lot of destruction."

"I bet it did," I say. Just looking at the ugly thing gives me eye cancer.

"My sister," Mel barks. "Where is she?"

"Relax. She's right here." He waves his hand, exposing the inside of said unicorn's belly and it isn't pretty.

"Faith!" The terror in Mel's voice rattles through my bones as she spots her sister, hurt and shackled in the pit of the unicorn's belly.

"Oh, would you hold your horses?" Abbadon says, running a hand through his wet hair, laughing about his own lame joke. "She's fine."

"Fine?" Mel's skin is set ablaze. "You call that

fine?"

Even I wouldn't refer to Faith's current state as fine. Her face is barely recognizable, for Satan's sake. Seriously, she looks as if she went toe to toe with hell's best boxers. (Gene and Max are no joke.) "What game are you playing?" I ask the bastard.

Abbadon shrugs. "Me? I'm not the one consorting with the witch I was tasked to kill."

"No," I reply flatly. "You're just the reason I was tasked with killing her."

"Honestly," he says. "I was kind of hoping she'd off you first, but one can't have everything, right?"

Mel shakes off her initial shock, allowing her wrath to consume her. "Let her go!"

"Of course," Abbadon says, snapping his fingers. A heartbeat later, the unicorn dissolves and the battered and bruised Faith drops to the cement floor.

Mel immediately runs toward her sister, pulling her out of Abbadon's reach. "I'm going to burn the flesh off your face for this."

Abbadon laughs. "I'd like to see you try, witch."

Something about this strikes me as wrong. Why would Abbadon abduct Faith and then just let her go? "Berith," I face my sister. "Take Faith out of here."

My sister knows me well enough not to question me right now and despite the doubt gleaming in her eyes, she follows my order. In a split second, she's next to Mel, grabbing hold of Faith. "I'll keep her safe," she promises Mel, who appears unsure if she should let my sister take care of her sister.

"Isn't that sweet?" Abbadon says.

Mel's hesitation ends right then and there. "Just make sure she's okay, will you?"

Berith lifts Faith and nods. "I will." Her gaze darts to me. "Make sure you repay the favor."

Mel flinches but nods. "I promise."

In the blink of an eye, Berith and Faith are gone, leaving us with Abbadon, who continues to grin as if he won the lottery.

"Game over," Mel says, allowing her flames to roar to life, to consume her body and soul.

"Game over," Abbadon parrots. "For you."

Before the weight of his words sinks in, I hear his thunderous voice. The very voice feared by heaven and hell alike. "Why is she still alive?"

My gaze darts over my shoulder to where my father stands, arms crossed, forehead wrinkled, eyes gleaming with rage. "What are you doing here?"

Abbadon grins. "I invited him."

"You did what?" I bark.

My father moves toward me. "See, son, Abbadon claimed that what you had with that thing"—he eyes Mel as if she's the monster—"weakened you. He said you are no longer faithful to me."

"Did he?" I snort, fists balled and ready to destroy the duke of destruction.

My father nods. "But I assured him he's wrong. He is, isn't he?"

# Chapter 25

*Melissani*

The king of hell also known as Beelzebub moves exactly like Lev. Like he owns the world and everyone in it. The power radiating off him is also eerily similar to Lev's. Just a bit stronger. And where Lev's eyes are the color of liquified emeralds his father's are a heavenly shade of blue. No clue how long I just stand there gaping at the king of all demons, but when he grabs Lev by the collar of his shirt, my fire roars like a damn lion. "You are my favorite," he says. "But I had to make sure you were still loyal."

The dark force inside me slams against its cage, forcing me to do something really stupid—to address the damn king of hell. "You played us."

His gaze remains on Lev. "I simply allowed Abbadon to prove his point."

"By pretending I abducted her sister?" Lev barks. "By sacrificing legions?"

The king shrugs. "Sacrifices are necessary, son. You should know that." He pauses. "Besides, those bastards were getting lazy. Had they kept their heads in the game she couldn't have ended them."

Lev shakes his head. "I don't believe you."

The king pulls him closer. "And I don't believe you." He nods in my direction. "I gave you an order. Yet she's still alive."

Verin approaches them. "Let's all just take a deep breath, okay?"

"We will," the king replies. "As soon as your brother kills the witch."

Verin, who didn't seem to mind killing me before, is paler than a ghost. "Father, why don't we talk about this? She—"

"Enough!" The king roars, pushing Lev toward me. "Kill her, now!"

Realization hits hard. Lev doesn't have a choice. It's either me or him and even when I loved him, I always knew what he'd do if he had to choose. "It's okay," I say, rolling my flames back and dropping to my knees. "We had a deal," I say, reminding him. He kept his end of the bargain, helping me save my sister. Now it's my turn to repay him. "I won't put up a fight."

Lev's eyes meet mine. An avalanche of emotions I'd never seen in him rolls through them. "I'm sorry," he whispers as a veil of pure darkness pours out of his palm.

"So sweet," Abbadon sighs, but I ignore him and close my eyes, waiting for Lev's magic to do what it was always meant to do—kill the half-breed witch and drag her to hell.

Moments tick by. Lev's darkness inches closer but the black smoke is so slow. I feel like I'm trapped in a time loop and despite my claims of not fearing death, I get twitchy. "Just kill me already," I bark.

"I…"

"Leviathan," his father thunders. "Now!"

Chapter 26

*Leviathan*

The darkness in my palm reaches out to Mel. The beast is hungry and out for blood. It longs for death and destruction. But seconds before it wraps around Mel's throat it…It stops. The hunger is still there, but there's something else banging against my chest. Something stronger than the beast, something that refuses to hurt Mel.

"Leviathan!" The disappointment in Father's voice is thick. "What are you waiting for?"

"I…" I close my eyes and the memory washing over me strikes true, like a knife to the damn heart.

\*\*\*\*

*"What are you doing here?" Mel hissed as she spotted me in the club. She worked the bar and though I had kept my distance, evidently, she felt my presence. Now on her break, she glared at me with crossed arms and a deep frown. "You know stalking is a crime, right?"*

*I leaned against the wall, grinning. "Princes don't stalk. We court, love."*

*"Yeah?" She rolled her eyes. "Then, why are you here? Surely, not to court me."*

*The gleam in her eyes intrigued me. It was a mixture of curiosity and animosity. Just like when she signed the deal her mother had made in her name. Just like on the rooftop when I found her stargazing.* "Would you believe me if I said I was nearby?"

"No."

"Meeting a friend?"

"No."

"Fine," I muttered. "How about I'm making sure my investment is taken care of?"

"Probably." She exhaled sharply. "As you can see." She pointed at herself. "Your investment is fine." She nodded at the exit. "You may go now."

I drank her in. She wore a tight, black shirt with the logo of a famous rock band, sneakers, and a black mini skirt. "Fine," I whispered, inching closer. "You are."

Mel took a step back. "What do you want?"

*You. I want you. And not just her soul, but her body, too.* "Why don't we get out of here?"

"Because I have a job," she muttered. "And thanks to you, I won't get a break today."

"Wrong," I replied, grabbing her wrist and pulling her toward the bar.

"What are you doing?" She struggled to free herself from my grip but that was pointless. "Hey, are you—"

I halted in front of the bar, facing her. "You had a job." Her lips parted, but I didn't give her a chance to object. Instead, I zoomed in on the other bartender and declared, "She quits."

"Are you insane?" Mel barked as I pulled her through the crowd toward the exit.

"A little," I replied as heat radiated from her skin. *The kind of heat I knew could end me and not just the vessel I grew rather attached to, but my essence as well. The thing was...I didn't care. There was something about the witch that made me reckless and wild. Something that led to stupid choices, like pushing her against the brick wall of the building to claim her lips.*

*I would relish the feel of her mouth on mine for centuries to come. And I'd never forget the slap that followed. She hit me so hard, my head jerked to the left. In hindsight, I was fairly certain that was the point of no return, the moment I decided I needed to make her mine—body, soul, and heart.*

\*\*\*\*

"Just do it," Mel pleads, her voice rough with desperation. "I'm okay with dying."

Maybe she was. But I wasn't okay with it. None of this was her fault. Had the roles been reversed and someone took one of my siblings...Well, let's just say there'd been hell to pay. So, why in Satan's name should I kill her? To prove I wasn't in love? That I was still loyal? "That's bullshit," I hiss, commanding the darkness back into my soul. "I'm not going to kill a witch as powerful as her to falsify that"—I shoot Abbadon a killer look—"bastard's claims."

"We are so fucked," Verin mutters as our father moves toward me.

"Are you disobeying me?" he asks, eyes narrow.

I nod. "Guess, I am."

"For a witch?"

"There's no need to kill her," I say, trying to justify my actions. "She—"

"She," Father roars. "Should have never been born. So, I'm giving you one last chance, Leviathan. Kill her, or I will have your head."

There's no doubt in my mind my father will go through with his threat, but it changes nothing. "I won't kill her."

Mel's eyes almost pop out of their sockets. "Are you fucking crazy? He's going to kill you, you idiot."

"Listen to her," Abbadon says, smirking. "She's smart."

I drop to one knee, taking her hands in mine. "I've lived a very long life, Mel. And you know what they say." I flash her my most charming smile. "All beauty must die."

That said, I feel my father's claws digging into the nape of my neck as he pulls me to my feet. "You, stupid bastard," he grunts. "You were my favorite."

His essence creeps into my body, making my insides burn with sharp pain. I've always known that one day I'd cease to exist, just never figured it'd be my own father ending me.

Chapter 27

*Melissani*
What is that stupid, arrogant idiot doing?
*Getting himself killed.*
Obviously. But why? Because he woke up today and all of a sudden decided to become the hero instead of the villain? Was he tired of being the crown prince of hell and figured...Hey, why not play the role of knight in shining armor for a change? And if so, didn't he get the memo—heroes save damsels in distress not wicked witches, for crying out loud. I mean, has he never watched one of those princess meets prince movies? Never read a damn fairytale?

His father's essence—a thick, dark, red smoke— wraps around Lev's throat, chocking the life out of him. The king of hell doesn't stop there. He pushes the ugly smoke into Lev's chest. His soul-shattering scream must be heard in all of hell.

What a stubborn, stupid prick!
*Why do you care? A few hours ago, you were going to be his reaper. So, what's your problem, Melissani?*
Berith's face flashes before my eyes. She made sure my sister was safe and asked me in return to do the same for her brother. But if I'm being honest to myself, Berith isn't the only reason I can't just stand here and watch him die. No matter how much he hurt me, there was a time when I loved him and he...He made me feel

like I mattered. Now, despite his warning outside the basilica, he wants to die for me? No. I won't let him. "Just kill me!" I yell at him. "Please, Lev!"

He meets my eyes with a half-smile, blood dripping from the corner of his mouth. "B-Begging d-doesn't suit you," he croaks, his voice broken and low.

My heart pounds against my chest and restricts my airway. "Lev!" I crawl toward him. "You can't do it! If you die, then what happens to my soul?"

"F-free," he stammers, barely able to keep his eyes open.

Abbadon smirks. "The two of you are disgustingly sweet." He faces the king and lowers his head. "But I think you should stop playing with him, brother." He sighs. "He is your son, so maybe you should grant him a quick end."

The king's blazing red eyes meet Lev's. "All of this for a useless witch whore," he spits at him, anger rolling through his voice, coloring the insidious smoke a darker, uglier shade of red. "Such a disappointment."

"Likewise," Lev retorts.

And that was the last straw for his father. He throws his head back, summoning his power. A power so potent it makes my insides burn and covers the whole place in a reddish gleam.

Verin wakes from his shock, turning to face me. "Do something," he pleads.

I want to. I swear, I would do anything to stop this madness. The question is what? What can I do to make him stop? Leviathan's father is Beelzebub, one of the first demons, a legend and currently the reigning king of hell. I'm powerful, for sure. But am I strong enough to take on Beelzebub?

*You have to try! He's dying, because of you. For you!*

I draw a deep breath, gather my chi, and force myself up. "Let him go," I demand of the ruler of all infernal regions. "Let him go now!"

The king laughs. "I don't fear you, witch."

I straighten my spine and hold my head up higher than ever before. I've done awful things. Not just because I wanted to save Faith. No, I could have killed those demons quickly. I tortured them instead. And why? Because I was a coward, afraid to admit—even to myself—that I too was part demon. Enough, though. I am brave enough, strong enough to follow the dark flame that burns from within. I can do this. Can push away my fears to stand against the king of hell, because I am not simply a witch. I am so much more than that. "But you should," I reply.

"I will end both of you," he warns.

"We'll see about that." I close my eyes and for the first time in my life, I take the shackles off the darkness inside me and welcome it with open arms.

Black and green flames flicker across my mind's eye. I watch them, rising higher and higher until—

I am the fire.

## Chapter 28

*Leviathan*

I glare at Mel. She's engulfed in green and black flames, burning brighter than I've ever seen her burn before. Her face is glowing, her eyes—one blacker than a starless night, one greener than the Amazonas itself—pierce my father's. She looks alive. Like a burning star moments before it extinguishes. "Let him go," she screams like a siren.

"I'll be right back," my father says, dropping me like a sack of potatoes.

My throat is sore, my vessel aches to the point where I can't tell which part hurts, but all I can think of is Mel. I mean, what the does she think she is doing? Has she lost her damn mind? There's no way she can defeat my father. She's just getting the both of us killed.

*Is she, though? Look at her!*

I do. I look at her and I feel her. The power erupting from her equals a roaring storm bound to destroy anything in its path. I…I have never seen anything like it and by the time her flames transform into a black and green dragon, facing my father, I realize I might have underestimated the witch.

Verin is next to me, helping me up. "You okay?"

My insides are charred, but other than that… "I'm okay."

Verin sighs. "I knew you couldn't kill her."

"You just have to rub it in, huh?"

My brother shrugs. "I guess so."

Father circles Mel like a vulture circling a cadaver. "Do you really think you can defeat me, witch?"

"I don't know," Mel says, eyeing Verin. "But I can stall you."

"What the hell is she talking about?" I ask confused.

"I'm sorry," Mel whispers as my father's gaze darts to us, realization hitting him hard.

I have no clue what's going on, until Verin grabs my wrist and blinks us out of Abbadon's unicorn hell.

# Chapter 29

*Melissani*

The instant Verin dematerializes with Lev I breathe a sigh of relief. And isn't it ironic? Less than 24-hours ago, I was the reaper outside Lev's door. I had spent weeks planning his end and it was going to be painful and cruel. I believed he took everything from me—my soul, my heart, and my sister—the prick had made me feel like I was nothing and I was hell-bent on getting what I came for—his pretty head on a silver plate. Now, look at me, saving the demon who misused everything I gave him and more. Pretty damn stupid, huh?

"Do you really think you can defeat me?" his father roars.

The power surging through my veins is intoxicating and wild. It could lay cities to ruin, but can it end the king of hell? "I guess, we are about to find out, huh?" Without warning, I concentrate all my power, pushing the fire inside me to its limit and fueling the dragon before me. Then, with all my might, I command the fiery beast to attack.

The king evades the first attack, but when the hellfire strikes out a second time, I catch his jeans, scorching his expensive pants.

He looks down at himself. "You're going to pay for this."

"Big time," Abbadon adds, grinning like the cat

that ate all the canaries.

I'd all but forgotten about the duke. Now, that he reminded me of his presence, I remember that I made a promise to myself. Whoever took Faith was going to pay for it with his life. "Maybe," I say, lifting my palm. "But you won't live to see it." When I drop my hand, the dragon flings itself at Abbadon. The poor bastard never saw his end coming. But I have to admit, I enjoy his painful screams a lot.

The king's confused gaze meets mine. "I should have never allowed you to live."

"Too late," I say, forcing the dragon to attack him again.

This time, however, I meet resistance. The king has unleashed his own beast—a monster with tentacles laced with razor blades and the head of a lion made of red smoke and fueled by unfiltered hate and rage. It's the biggest, scariest thing I've ever seen. "Tonight," he says, flashing me a brilliant smile. "You will die, little witch." The beast inches closer and I take a step back. "And once I'm done with you, I'll find my useless son and make him wish he'd never met you."

"Pretty sure he already does." Wish he'd never met me, I mean. But what's done is done and even the crown prince of hell can't turn back the hands of time.

Beelzebub sighs. Then, a second later he lifts his hand, and the ugly beast comes at me. Hard.

# Chapter 30

*Leviathan*

"What the fuck did you do?" I yell at Verin as the familiar walls of the mausoleum blink into existence. Pain shoots through my vessel and I can still feel my father's darkness, taking root in my bones, but none of that matters because my brother brought me back to the cemetery, brought me back from hell and...And left Mel on her own to battle my father.

"I saved your sorry ass," he replies. "And you're welcome."

He did save me. I should be grateful, should be happy to be alive and kicking. I just...I can't. "You sentenced her to death," I bark, close to pulling my hair out.

"No," Verin says, voice stern, eyes locked on mine. "You did, the second you fell in love with her."

"I don't love her!" For the love of Lucifer, I'm a demon, the crown prince of hell. I don't love anyone but myself.

Verin laughs. "You would have died for her."

*I would have.* "I still don't love her." I might be a bit obsessed with her, I'm demon enough to admit that. But love? Love is for prince charming, not for the future ruler of hell.

Verin puts a hand on my shoulder. "Are you trying to convince me or yourself, brother?"

I don't know, but what I do know is, "I can't let her die." The instant she pulled herself up to face my father, she signed her own death certificate. The worst part? She knew it. She was well aware of the consequences of her decision. Yet she chose me. She chose to save the demon who bought her soul from her own mother, who knowingly ruined her. She was going to give her life for the creature who tossed her on the street like a bag of trash, the very creature who assured her he could never love a witch like her. Dear Satan, I'm such an asshole.

Verin rolls his eyes. "You can't defeat him, brother."

"Watch me," I roar as I walk back through the portal, straight into my own hell.

## Chapter 31

*Melissani*

The tentacles of the smoke-monster reach for me from every side. I stand tall, keep all of my energy focused on the fire-dragon, standing between that thing and me. "Push. Back," I order and when I close my eyes, I put everything I've got into it.

My fire burns and while the dragon keeps the beast at bay, I allow one of the black flames to escape. Like a snake it slithers across the ground. The king is so focused on the dragon, he never saw the tiny fire snake coming.

"What the—" He doesn't get to finish the sentence. The snake is already wrapping itself around his fine leather shoes, working its way up.

He stills and for a brief second, I revel in the illusion that maybe…Just maybe I can defeat him. Sure, he is one of the oldest and most powerful demons, but he hasn't seen a battlefield in ages and that makes him lazy and arrogant.

The snake slithers up his leg, setting his left side on fire. He screams like a baby brought into this world covered with blood and about to leave it drenched in the very liquid that gave him life.

"You little bitch," he barks, his eyes not blue but the darkest shade of red I've ever seen. "How dare you?" He lifts his fingers, snapping them. A heartbeat later, the snake explodes into a million tiny sparks. It looks like a Fourth of July firework except I've got no reason to celebrate. Nope, none whatsoever. He snaps his fingers again and his left side looks as if it never burned. It's in this very moment, I realize game over.

He extends his arms and pushes the monster forward. My dragon retreats, still trying to cover me but unable to fight off the tentacles. "I loved these shoes," he says, grinning. "Thanks to you, they're ruined." He shakes his head and sighs. "Grave mistake, little witch."

From the corner of my eye, I spot a tentacle. It's too late. By the time, my brain processes the image, the thing is already slicing my thigh open.

Blood oozes out of the wound.

The sick pain forces me to my knees.

My insides burn...Burn as if—

Another tentacle comes for me. This one aims for my heart. I barely manage to turn my upper body and it slices my back instead.

More pain. More blood.

Again and again, the thing strikes.

Again and again, it slices through my skin.

More and more blood covers the ground.

Eventually, I lose focus and the fire rolls back into my soul, leaving me at the king of hell's mercy without any protection. And while I'm lying on the cold hard ground, blood pouring out of my nose, my ears, and countless wounds the king orders his beast back, caging it inside his rotten essence. It isn't needed anymore. I am in no shape to fight back. And the asshole knows it. "I can see why Leviathan fell for you." He kneels beside me, brushing my bloody hair off my damaged face. "You're beautiful and strong. But I can't allow a liaison like that. It's too dangerous."

I manage a half-hearted smile. "For whom?"

He leans in. "For me." His fingers wrap around my throat, forcing the life out of me. That's when I spot movement out of the corner of my eye.

"Let her go!" Lev's voice sends a wave of warmth over my skin. He came back. Why the fuck did he come back?

The king keeps strangling me, grinning at his son. "Did you decide to die an honorable death, son?"

"No," Lev replies. "I decided to gain my inheritance a little early." Then he pushes his darkness out, aiming it right at his father.

The king lets go of me, but before he can strike back, the earth beneath us starts shaking. "What the—"

"You fucked with the wrong witches," Faith's voice echoes off the walls as the earth opens up, carving an abyss into the ground.

What happens next is nothing but a blur. Someone—I think Berith—lifts me. Another one— Verin—grabs Lev and Faith and then…

Then we're back in the mausoleum and Berith seals the portal to hell shut with her blood.

# Chapter 32

*Leviathan*

I move toward Mel. Faith is kneeling behind her, holding her head in her lap. She's in real bad shape. Her body is...A battlefield. The wounds my father inflicted upon her should have killed her. Had she been human, she would have died on our way to the mausoleum. "Are you okay?"

She ogles me like I'm the one who went toe to toe with the king of hell. And I sort of did, just differently. "I'm fine," she mutters. "I mean, I'm not the one who lost his damn mind." Still snarky, but I'm not nearly dumb enough to fall for her lies. Her voice is broken, barely above a whisper and her pain-stricken expression says more than any words ever could.

*She could still die!* The annoying voice inside my head is right, but I can't let myself consider the possibility of losing her. So, I shut the voice out and narrow my eyes at her. "What's that supposed to mean?"

"It means..." She draws what looks like an incredibly painful breath. "You should have just killed me."

I smile. "And where's the fun in that?"

She shakes her head. Or at the very least, she tries to. "Is everything a game to you, Lev?" Sparks ignite in her eyes. "I mean, what do you think happens now?

Your father doesn't strike me as the forgiving type."

"He's not," Berith says.

Verin nods. "We are officially on Hell's Most Wanted list."

"So, we're officially dead?" Faith asks, sighing heavily.

"Yup," Verin replies.

"Bullshit." I run my hand down Mel's cheek, wiping off some of the blood. "The crown prince of hell, the princess of hell, the prince of hell, a hellfire witch and an earth witch," I say. "I'd say the odds are in our favor."

"So, you said the last time," Mel says.

"And we're still alive, aren't we?"

"Yeah." She coughs up blood. "The question is for how long?"

I'm all set to give her the pep talk of a lifetime. (Contrary to what you may believe I am a fantastic motivational speaker. Why do you think the best of the best in that field made contracts with me?) So, I'm all set to bring it on when out of the blue Mel's eyes roll back. Next thing I know, Faith screams her sister's name, "Mel! Mel! Wake up!"

She shakes her.

Shakes her real hard.

Her eyes remain shut.

## Chapter 33

*Melissani*

"Faith?" She screams my name and sounds so much like our mother, it's kind of creepy. "Faith, I'm here. Where are you?"

It's so dark I can't see shit.

"Melissani!" Lev's voice is distant, like the whispering of the ocean when you press a shell to your ear. "Melissani, open your eyes. Now!"

*Are my eyes closed? Is that why it's so dark?*

"Please," he begs. "Please, open your eyes."

*I'm trying, prick.* It's just...I swear, my eyes are already open. I can feel my lashes beating against my eyelids when I blink.

"Me—" Lev's voice is barely a whisper. Then, it's gone.

I spin and try to get an idea of where I am, but I lose my balance and plop on my butt. The flooring is cold. Feels like cement or stone. I steady myself, putting most of my weight on my palms, and draw a painful breath. Goddess, my insides are on fire. And not the kind of fire I'm used to. It's a low simmering burn, a sharp, pulsating pain rippling through my bones and every fiber of my being. The king's monster did a real number on me. Quite frankly, I'm not sure how I'm still alive. I lost so much blood I could have fed an entire vampire army. Fine, not an army, but enough vamps to overrun a small town. Still, I can't help but feel like the blood loss is the least of my problems.

Vivid memories flash before my eyes. I'm back at Abbadon's place. From the sideline, I watch the tentacled beast slice through my thigh. I remember the first cut best. The odd feeling that rushed through my veins. *Like poison.* It felt as if the razor-sharp blades on the beast's tentacles had been laced with witch hazel.

*Is that why I'm in so much pain? Was I poisoned?*

I close my eyes and try to make sense of what's going on.

*Where am I? Where are the others? And why am I still alive? Wait, am I? Alive, I mean?*

Panic pushes its sharp claws into my chest.

*Did I die? Is this—*

I yank my eyes open and stare into the darkness.

*Is this where souls go after they take their last breath?*

That doesn't really make sense, does it? My soul belongs to Leviathan, so if I were dead, shouldn't I go straight to—

*To where? Where does my soul go after I die?*

That question came out wrong. Of course, I'm aware of where my soul will eventually end up. See, Leviathan is a business demon through and through and before I signed that deal, he gave me a rather long and boring speech about the fate of witches dumb enough to sell their souls. It went something like, "You'll die, your soul will be reaped, your body will be preserved, you'll join my other priceless trophies bound to do what I say, when I say it." In short, he prepared me for a life as his slave. What he neglected to mention was how the whole reaping part worked. Would my soul go to purgatory for a while? Would I be stuck in some sort of limbo? I have no clue. I never asked him either. What can I say? The future looked dire, and I didn't feel like getting into details. Still, it seems rather unlikely for a marked soul to end up here, surrounded by impenetrable darkness and bone-chilling silence. Or maybe, I just want it to be unlikely, because deep down I don't want to be dead.

Whatever it is, I've got to figure it out. Preferably sooner rather than later. Because I am afraid of the dark.

## Chapter 34

*Leviathan*

"Mel!" If she were a Siren, Faith's piercing screams would rupture the stone walls of the mausoleum. The power radiating from her shakes the earth and is about to cause some real damage.

I share her desperation, feel her pain, but bringing the mausoleum down isn't going to save Mel. "Faith." I grab her hand. "You've got to calm down."

Her gaze darts to me. "Don't you dare," she says, her anger rising like a thick blanket of black smoke. "This is your fault! All of this!" She digs her nails in Mel's shoulders and shakes her some more. "Please, Mel. Wake up."

The ground shakes again, ever so slightly. If Faith doesn't pull it together, we'll be buried in this grave. Ironic, huh?

"Does she have a pulse?" Berith asks, slowly approaching Faith.

I wish I knew, but Faith won't let me near her and I'm afraid she might cause a deadly earthquake if I force her aside. "Faith," I try again, keeping the anger out of my voice. "Please, let me check on her."

She shakes her head. "You've done enough."

If I had a heart and if I suffered from a guilty conscience, I'd say she's right. When I saw Mel in that stupid bar in New York, when I watched her burn preppy-boy's fingers, I sealed the witch's fate. I had to have her consequences be damned. It's why I agreed to her mother's deal, despite knowing how wrong it was to make a deal with someone who was literally forced to sign it. Back then, I just…I didn't care. I wanted her. So, I took her. Now, she's lying in a grave, dying. (Fabulous job, Leviathan. I'm so proud of you.) Well, luckily, I don't have a heart and a guilty conscience is nothing but a myth to me. "Faith!" I shift a bit closer. "Let me try to help her. I promise I won't hurt her. I just want to help."

Finally, I have her attention. She inhales sharply, lifts her head, ignores the salty liquid running down her cheeks and barks, "How? How can you help her?" She runs a hand down Mel's face. "Even you can't bring back the dead, Leviathan." (That's arguable. I have fantastic connections to the reaper world and know quite a few gifted necromancers.)

But I don't need to contact any of them just yet. "She isn't," I say.

Faith narrows her eyes. "How can you be so sure?"

I sigh. "Because her soul belongs to me, remember?" I would know if a reaper had taken her. "She's not dead. Yet." *But she is slowly dying.* "So, please, I'm begging you." Our gazes meet. "Let me check her."

She considers me, visibly battles with her own doubts and fears. Eventually, hope wins. "If you hurt her—"

"I won't," I promise, nodding at Verin to come over.

"What do you need?" he asks, eyeing Mel's lifeless body.

I point to Faith. "Make sure she's okay." If anything were to happen to her sister, Mel would kill me.

Verin sighs. "Come on." He gently puts his hands around Faith shoulders and pulls her up. "Let him try to save her."

This time the earth-witch doesn't put up a fight. She allows Verin to guide her away from Mel.

I finally get a chance to check her pulse. It takes a second, then I feel it. Her heart is still beating. Barely. "She's alive," I say, trying to be reassuring.

Berith kneels down next to me, inspecting the wounds our father inflicted upon her. "Look at that," she says, pointing to the long cut on her thigh. "Is that—"

"Fuck," I bark.

"What?" Faith struggles against Verin's grip. "What is it?"

My heart races. "Witch hazel," I whisper, never taking my eyes off the blackening veins around the cut. "My father poisoned her with witch hazel."

Berith bites her lower lip. "A lot of it." She eyes the other wounds. "Judging from the look of it, she shouldn't be breathing anymore."

"But she is," I bark. "And that means we can still save her."

"How?" Verin shakes his head. "There's no antidote, is there?"

"There is," Faith says. "But…" She trails off, her eyes growing heavy with sorrow.

"What?" I demand. "What is it?"

"There's only one person who knows how to prepare the antidote," she says, voice weak.

I get on my feet. "Then, let's go."

She shakes her head. "We can't."

"Why?" I yell, close to strangling her.

"Two reasons," Faith replies, tears streaming down her cheeks. "One: I'm pretty sure she won't help us. My mother screwed her over once and she's not been a fan ever since. Two: she lives in New Orleans, and I don't think Mel will make the trip."

Damn! New Orleans? "That's what a three-hour trip?"

Verin already fiddles with his phone. "Two hours and forty minutes."

"Still," Berith says. "Faith is right. She won't make it." Her gaze darts over the blackened veins. "The poison is spreading too fast."

I tilt my head, facing my brother. "We can blink her to New Orleans or use a portal."

"Are you crazy?" Berith shakes her head. "We're on Hell's Most Wanted List."

"The second we use our magic the boss will be able to trace us," Verin adds as if I needed the explanation, as if I weren't aware of what our father can and cannot do. He taught me everything I know about being a demon.

Berith rests her hand on my shoulder. "I'm sorry, Lev. But—"

"No!" I won't listen. Not even for a second. Mel is still alive, she's still breathing. "We've got to try." I can't just sit here and watch her die.

*Why not? Her soul will come back to you after she takes her last breath.*

Yes, her soul will be mine, but Mel wouldn't be Mel anymore. She'd have to obey me. She'd have to play by my rules. She'd have to do whatever I want her to do. And that would be—

*Amazing?*

Boring as hell.

"She will make it," I promise them.

"Lev," Berith whispers softly. "You—"

I shake her hand off. "Step aside, Berith."

"What are you doing?" Verin asks, knowing me all too well.

I ignore the question and pull the bone-dagger out of its holster on my back. This isn't the end. Not yet. I brush sticky, bloody strands out of Mel's face. "You'll be okay," I say, before I slice the dagger through my palm, face the south and say, *"Tenetur in vita. In morte tenetur. Sit vita tua sit essential vitae essentia."*

"Lev!" Berith's eyes go wide. "What are you doing? Don't!"

Too late. My blood is already dripping into Mel's mouth, connecting my life essence to hers.

"What did you do?" Faith asks. The shock drained all the color from her face.

"He bound his life to hers," Verin explains, shaking his head in defeat.

Faith stares at me with an unhinged jaw. "You did what?"

I'm not in the mood to explain my actions. Instead, I put the dagger away, put my hands under Mel's body and lift her. "Let's go. We don't have forever." As a matter of fact, I'm not sure we have three hours. My father must have used enough of the poison to kill a hundred witches and I already feel the effect of the spell, it drains me to the point where lifting Mel feels like lifting the Empire State Building.

Chapter 35

*Melissani*

My steps echo through the blackness. Other than that, it's awfully quiet. Too quiet. I feel lost, like I'm trapped in the Minotaur's labyrinth, bidding my time until the blood-hungry creature finally decides to attack.

"Hello?" I sound like a broken record, repeating the same words over and over, hoping someone eventually answers.

No one does.

"Can someone hear me?"

Nothing.

Except the echo of my own pitiful voice.

"Is anybody here?" I try again.

No reply.

Goddess, what is this godforsaken place? And why am I here? One minute, I spoke to Lev and the next...It was dark. "That's some fucked-up shit," I mutter to myself. I mean, it would totally suck if I had died. But if I am dead...Well, I'd like to know. At least, I could come to terms with it then. Wandering around aimlessly, not knowing where I am are or what happened, is a fate worse than death.

"Hello!" I shout again.

"Hello!" The echo off my voice comes back, except...It doesn't sound like my voice.

"Who's there?" I shout, fear digging a hole through

my chest. "Show yourself!"

"Not yet," the voice that's mine and yet isn't replies. "You've got a bit of time left. Enjoy it."

Enjoy it? How am I supposed to enjoy anything in this shithole of blackness? And what the hell does "a bit of time left" mean? Time for what? Is there a countdown I'm unaware of? And if so, what is it counting down to? "Hey! Talk to me! Where am I? Who are you?"

This time when the echo returns it's my desperate voice and nothing else. Great. Just great.

## Chapter 36

*Leviathan*

I—Leviathan, Crown Prince of Hell, and ruler of 777 infernal regions, Prince of Envy (That's a myth. I have never met anyone who was better than moi, so how could I be envious?)—am sitting in the backseat of a stolen Mercedes, cradling a dying witch. A dying witch, whose life is now bound to my own. Which means Mel isn't the only one dying in the backseat of this tacky car. I too am about to pay purgatory an eternal visit. Satan, this feels like the end of the world, surreal and mad. Or maybe I'm just insane. Why else would I have connected my essence to hers?

"Brother?" Verin eyes me through the rear-view mirror of the car that Faith, of all people, stole. "You don't look so good. Are you okay?"

A ton of poison is washing through me. So okay is not exactly the term I'd use to describe my current situation. Verin doesn't need to know, though. He needs to keep his eyes on the road and get us to New Orleans as fast as possible. "Really?" I force a smile. Lifting my lips hurts. "And here I thought I was the most handsome of all the devils."

Berith nudges me. She's been quietly sitting beside me, watching me like a hawk. "Drop the act, Lev." She points to my neck. "The poison is spreading uncontrollably."

I don't need a reminder. I feel the effect of the witch-hazel. It's almost as painful as my father's essence when it ripped through my cells. Burns like hell really. And I can't help but wonder how Mel is still breathing? Witch-hazel isn't toxic to demons, which means I feel only half of what Mel must. The spell I used slows down her approaching end. Kind of like slow-motion in a movie. Yet it's inevitable and I can see and feel it drawing closer. She grows weaker by the second and soon the toxin will take her life and...Well, my life, too. The spell allowed me to transfer some of my life-force into Mel, giving us a bit more time to get the antidote. But if we don't make...Well, let's just say, the spell works both ways. Meaning, if she dies, I die. It's as simple as that. But that won't happen. It can't.

"So, who is the ominous woman that can cure her?" I ask, changing the topic.

Faith's gaze drops to her folded hands resting in her lap. "Most refer to her as the Queen of New Orleans."

"I thought Marie Laveau was dead," Verin mutters, referring to one of the most powerful mambas the world had ever known. (She was also a great entertainer and I used to enjoy her company greatly. Well, until she realized who I was and then banished me back to hell. That was not nice at all.)

Faith sighs. "She is."

"But?" Verin pushes.

"Her great-great-great granddaughter isn't."

Berith narrows her eyes, sudden understanding flickering across her face. "Are we talking about Josephine Lacroix?"

Faith turns to my sister. "You know her?"

Berith draws a long deep breath. "You could say that."

"Did we miss something?" Verin asks, speeding down the highway like a racecar driver.

Berith bites her cheek and gazes out the window. Trees flit past us and she grows distant. For a while, she says nothing. Then she replies, "War. You missed a bloody war."

I want to ask her what she's talking about, but Mel starts twitching and jerking.

"What is happening?" Faith asks, fear strangling her voice.

Mel's skin is ice cold and even if my life weren't bound to hers and I couldn't feel the pain slicing through my chest, I'd know. "She's running out of time." I pull her closer. "You've got to drive faster," I order Verin.

His gaze darts to the dashboard. "Any faster and we're flying."

"Just go!" I bark.

# Chapter 37

*Melissani*

A faint noise vibrates through the everlasting darkness. It sounds like heavy fabric being dragged along the floor.

"Who's there?" I croak, well aware someone or something is drawing closer.

*BAM.*

*BAM.*

*BAM.*

Heavy footsteps echo off the walls. Whoever or whatever it is…It's big and probably strong.

A pulse of energy jolts through my beaten body, alerting me to its presence. A very, very powerful presence if the raised hairs on the back of my neck aren't mistaken.

"Show yourself," I bark yet again.

A sigh follows. "Are you sure that's what you want?"

*I don't know. Am I?* I have no clue where I am or what creature I'm sharing this godless place with. And while the pain slicing through every inch of my being is slowly fading (or maybe I'm just fading), the fear grows. It's so weird. I feel like…I don't know. Like I'm floating, as if I'm losing control over my body, because my soul is being pulled out of it. So, yeah. I am sure I need to know what the hell is going on with me. "Who are you?"

"I have many names," comes the quick reply.

*Super helpful, dude!* "Could you be any more ominous?" I mean, just because I'm trapped in…Whatever this is, doesn't mean I'm into cryptic messages. It just makes this whole shit-show creepier. And I have had my fair share of creepy today. I went to Abbadon's hellish unicorn kingdom, located in a parallel dimension inside Vatican City. If that isn't creepy, then what is?

"I could indeed be more specific," the thunderous voice replies, sounding less and less like my own. "But I doubt you'd like the details. On the contrary, I'm certain you would not enjoy the truth."

*Enjoy!* Ha! There's that stupid word again. "Can anyone enjoy this?"

"A valid question." The footsteps grow louder. The sound of a heavy coat brushing over stone sends chills down my spine. "Perhaps, if one were to thrive on pain and suffering."

Goddess, this is so messed up. I'm also done with this madness. "All right, can we drop the bullshit? Who are you and what am I doing here?"

"I am…" He pauses, for dramatic effect perhaps? "The end. And you, my dear Melissani, are dying."

"I'm what?" Did he just imply he's death and I'm…I'm about to bite the dust?

"Relax," he says, calmly. "You're not dead. *Yet.*"

"Yet?" *Does that mean*…No! I refuse to finish that thought. "Dude, whoever or whatever you are, will you please stop talking in riddles and get to the point?" I'm sort of losing it here and I'm not just talking about my damn mind but my body, too.

"The point?" he (sounds like a man, at least) parrots. "Well, what is the point, dear Melissani? What is the purpose of life and the reason for all the pain and suffering?" He laughs as if he just cracked the joke of the century. "Let me know if you figure it out."

Jesus, what the hell? "If you're really death, you totally suck at it."

"I am not *the* death," he says. "I am merely one of many."

"Again, with the riddles." I sigh. "Aren't you growing tired of coming up with that shit?"

"No." His breath beats against my cheek, he's that close. "One needs a hobby if eternity is your companion, don't you think?"

"What I think—" I cut myself off before I make yet another mistake and insult "one of many deaths."

"Pray tell." He laughs again. "I'm very curious."

I shake my anger off. "Look, I'm really tired and I'd appreciate it if you could just tell me what's happening."

"As I said." Fabric rustles, it sounds like he's smoothing out wrinkles. "You're dying."

"And you're here to reap me?"

"That depends," he answers.

"On what?"

"On whether your demon will be successful or not."

My demon? Lev? But... "What is he doing?"

A bell rings. "I'm sorry, my dear Melissani. Work beckons. I'll be back in a heartbeat."

"No!" I shout, another, deeper kind of fear taking root in my heart. "Tell me what Lev is up to. Please!"

There's no reply.

He's gone.

Vanished into thin air.

And I'm left in the dark to wonder what stupid plan the demon came up with. I surely hope it doesn't involve Faith. If she gets hurt, I'll find my way back to deep fry the prick, even if I have to fight one of many deaths to do just that.

Chapter 38

*Leviathan*
Verin races through New Orleans. Flying past blurry street signs and lights. No clue how but he got us to the city of monsters and magic in less than two hours, but he did and it's a miracle no lawman stopped us. He must have broken at least a dozen laws. Granted, human laws. However, I don't think we could have argued with the police about only abiding by hell's laws. (Fine, we could have. But it would have surely ended in bloodshed, and I have had enough of that today.)

"Okay, so where are we headed?" Verin asks Faith.

She casts him a really-you-have-to-ask look. "The French Quarter, where else?" Can't say I blame her for being annoyed. Even humans know that when looking for magic the French Quarter is the place to go.

"You okay?" Berith asks.

I grow weaker by the second, which means Mel is losing the fight with the witch-hazel. So, no. I'm not okay. "Splendid."

"You don't look so splendid," Faith remarks.

"I always look splendid," I retort, because coming back at her with a snarky (but also very true) remark takes my mind off the inevitable truth—Mel is dying and so am I. Funny how the "so am I" part doesn't bother me as much as the "Mel is dying" part.

Chapter 39

*Melissani*

As promised, the shapeless voice returns quickly. Faster than I expected, to be honest. Who am I lying to? Faster than I wanted. Because this…Thing…Is death. Even if it proclaims to be one of many. It's still one of many deaths and since I'm not too keen on dying, I can't say I enjoy the company. The irony of it all is not lost on me. This one time I want to be alone, this one time I'm enjoying the hollow hole of loneliness in my chest, I'm in the company of death. Yay me!

"It's dull, isn't it?" he says, his voice bouncing off the everlasting darkness.

"It's better than a basilica full of unicorns and kitten stuff," I reply.

He chuckles. "I see you haven't lost your humor yet."

"I guess not." But I wasn't really joking either. Abbadon's place creeped me out. It reminded me of old witch stories about child demons and how they are obsessed with dolls. Apparently, they spent most of their nights raiding houses, looking for fancy new toys. After I listened to that story, I tossed all of Faith's dolls in the trash bin outside our house and forbid my mother to buy her new ones. My sister hated me fiercely after that. Her hate I could handle. A bunch of demonic kids stealing her dolls? Not so much. I lean against a cold surface, probably a wall or something. I really can't tell. It's just too dark and add, "But when life gives you lemons—"

"You ask for tequila," he finishes my sentence.

"Pretty much."

Another quiet moment passes between us, stretching for what feels like half an eternity. Then his footsteps resound in the dark and his unique energy penetrates my skin, rattling my bones. I can't stand the silence, so I cut through it. "So, you're death, huh?"

"One of many," he clarifies.

"A reaper then?"

"If that's what you'd like to call me."

"Why don't you show yourself?" I'm about to die. It would be the nice thing to do. You know, at least I'd get to look the end in the eye. Like a true warrior, not some coward who shuts their eyes, waiting for the battle to cease.

"I doubt you'd appreciate the face of death." He sighs. "Most people don't."

"I'm not most people," I shoot back. "And frankly, the darkness isn't exactly beautiful."

"No," he says as his signature energy draws closer. "I guess it's not."

A loud snap makes me jump. Next thing I know, I spot the light of a candle. It's dim and can't battle the utter darkness on its own, but it illuminates a large shadowy figure, wearing something that looks like a thick cloak and an old-fashioned top-hat.

"Better?" he inquires.

"Much," I admit. "Thank you."

"My pleasure, Melissani." He tilts his head, studying me closely. "Why don't you take a seat? This might take a little longer than I anticipated."

"Sit where?" I laugh.

"My bad." He snaps his fingers and out of the blue a comfy-looking armchair materializes next to me.

"That's a handy power," I say, slightly impressed. "Could have used it when I moved into my first apartment." I was only seventeen and could barely afford rent, let alone furniture. By the time I moved out, I owned a shabby second-hand mattress and a set of chairs for a dining room table I never bought.

He laughs and despite the fact he's a reaper waiting for my death, the sound warms my cold chest. "It's not easy living amongst humans, is it?"

I take a seat and shrug. "Nothing about life is easy."

"Neither is death," he says.

I look around, drinking in the darkness. "I guess not."

The shadowy figure inches a bit closer, and the light of the candle reflects in a dark set of eyes. They appear to be the darkest brown I'd ever seen. Almost black but not quite.

"So," I say, averting my gaze. "Do all your clients get this kind of service?"

"Only the VIPs," he replies.

I snort. "What an honor."

"It is," he says, his tone dead serious. (No pun intended.)

Having small talk with a reaper isn't exactly the weirdest thing I've ever done, but I'm tired of playing games and my mind races with questions I'd like answered before I take my very last breath. So, I take a shot in the dark—literally—and ask, "Why am I not dead yet?" I'm not an idiot. The witch hazel should have killed me by now. It was too much of it and in hindsight, I should have probably mentioned it to Lev or Faith when we returned to the mausoleum, but it all happened so fast and at the time I had other worries. Like how to make sure my sister would survive the king's revenge. Anyway, the point is, I have so much witch hazel in my system, I should have long perished.

The figure remains quiet.

"Don't you think I deserve an answer?" I laugh and quite honestly sound like a mad woman on the brink of insanity. "I'm dying, remember?"

"But you're not dead yet," he retorts. "And that is a question I cannot answer."

"Why?"

"Because it's not my place."

"Then who's is it?"

He draws a deep breath and after a moment says, "You should ask your demon boyfriend."

"He's not my boyfriend," I bark.

"Whatever you need to tell yourself, my dear Melissani."

*Can you strangle death?* Probably not. So, I move on to the next question. "Does every soul end up here before they die?"

"No," he replies. "Only the ones whose fates haven't been determined yet."

Again, with the ominous shit. "Could you elaborate?"

"This place"—he waves his shadowy hands around, gesturing at our surroundings—"is what we refer to as the waiting room."

"The waiting room for death?" I'd laugh if it didn't

sound so absurd.

He nods. "It's reserved for those who still have a chance to return."

Wait, did he just say... "Are you saying I might survive?"

"There's a chance," he says. "A very, very slim chance. But still."

"How?"

He sighs. "That's another question I cannot answer."

Jesus, how can death be so frustrating? All right, that might have been a stupid question. "Do you always wait with those souls?"

"I don't," he admits. "But as I said you are special."

"Why?" I don't feel special. I feel stupid.

He regards me silently. "Because I sincerely hope you will survive."

"You do?" I have a hard time believing that. "Why?"

He walks toward me, holding the candle away from his face, so I can't make out what's hidden under that stupid cloak and hat. "Would you care to see for yourself?" he asks, extending his hand. Which is really just a shadow of a hand.

"I..." Shouldn't. He's a reaper for crying out loud. Nothing good can come out of touching him, right?

"Don't be afraid," he says softly.

I can't tell whether it's my desperation, the need to do something other than sit around and wait for my death or the warmth his proximity brings. Either way, I take his hand and hope deep down I live to regret the choice.

Chapter 40

*Leviathan*

"In one hundred meters, the destination is on your right," the Mercedes' fancy GPS system babbles. Followed by, "You have arrived at your destination. The destination is on the right."

Faith had previously punched in the address for the ominous Josephine Lacroix and is now desperately trying to silence the annoying voice by slamming her fist against the on-board computer.

"Your destination is—"

"Shut up!" Faith silences her with one last hit and that one makes the whole screen go black. "Goddess, so annoying."

Verin smirks. "So, anger issues run through the family, huh?"

She casts him a single look. (One that might even intimate someone as fearless as myself.) She unbuckles her seatbelt and climbs out of the car wordlessly.

"She likes you," Berith jokes.

Verin shakes his head. "Witches."

Any other day, I'd happily join my sister in making Verin's life miserable. Today, though, I don't feel like my usual awesome self. Perhaps because I'm dying. But hey, I'm not the whiney type. Anyway, I gather my strength, open the door, and lift Mel's limp body out into the brutal New Orleans morning sun.

It's early spring, but the humidity and the heat are awful. Within seconds, I'm drenched in sweat. "So, where is she?"

Faith points to the town house on the right. It's an epitome of New Orleans French Quarter style and décor. "That's it," she says, ogling the terracotta façade as if it were a rattlesnake about to strike.

I want to ask the witch what kind of beef her mother has with this Josephine woman, but the poison does a great job of messing with my balance and so I stumble backward against the car.

Berith casts me a sidelong glance. If I didn't know better, I'd go as far as to say she looks worried. "Maybe you should wait in the car."

I shake my head. Or I think I do. "She needs the antidote. Now." We both do.

Faith turns to her sister. She glares at her lifeless face in defeat. "We made it so far."

"We did," I confirm.

"But…" She bites her thumbnail. "I hate to say it. I really do but…"

"Get to the point," I snap. (I think it's crucial to understand I do not usually snap at women. They are heaven and hell's gifts to…Well, to everyone and everything. But this bloody toxin clouds my brain and I'm running out of courtesy.)

"I don't think she's going to help us," Faith finally admits.

Berith squints. "I have met her and her children," my sister says. "And the Lacroixs didn't strike me as the kind of people who would let a fellow witch die."

I really want to know how my sister knows the woman, but I'm too exhausted to ask. Instead, I try to draw a deep breath—fail miserably—and point at the door. "She will help us." She won't have a choice because Mel's life depends on it. "So, let's get this over with, shall we?"

Verin, who has been awfully quiet up until now, sighs. "I hate witches."

"She's not a witch," Berith says, correcting him. "She's the voodoo high-priestess of New Orleans, brother. And from what I saw, you'd be smart not to fuck with her." The warning in Berith's voice rings loud and clear. "Oh," she adds, pressing her finger against her temple. "And one more thing. Don't mess with her kids either. One of them can send your sorry ass straight back to the pit without much effort."

"Great," Verin murmurs. "That's just great."

"A little help," I grumble. She's a light weight, but I can hardly carry myself, let alone the both of us.

Verin appears at my side. "I've got her."

"Thanks."

He eyes me, a touch of worry in his eyes. "You're freaking me out, man."

"Because I thanked you?" He nods. "Would you prefer I insulted you?"

"I would, actually."

"Fine, then move your lazy ass, you idiot." I sigh. "We don't have all day."

"Much better," he says, carrying Mel toward the building.

There are several condos and a bunch of young mambas—their scent is unique—gather on the balcony. One of them, a girl with curly black hair and a super sweet smile, approaches Faith, who leads the way. "Can I help you?"

"We're looking for the queen," she replies, her voice tainted with exhaustion and desperation alike.

The girl cocks a brow. "The queen lives in England."

"Look, I don't have time for this bullshit." Faith steps aside, giving the girl a view of Mel. The toxin has colored the veins in her neck black and she's so pale, she looks dead already.

"Shit," the girl barks, stumbling backward. "What the hell happened to her?"

"My sister is dying," Faith retorts. "So, you can either show us to the queen or—" I guess, she wanted to threaten her, but she can't seem to get any more words out, except a barely audible, "Please."

The girl nods. "Follow me."

She guides us to one of the dark green doors and points to a wooden bench. "Wait here," she orders, never taking her eyes off Mel. "I'll get her."

"Hurry," Berith adds, watching me from the corner of her eye.

The girl nods and disappears around the corner.

"Sit down," Berith orders me and I'm too tired to fight her.

Faith takes the seat next to me. She gazes at the metal railing and for a while she stares straight ahead. Then, she turns to me and says, "Why?"

"Come again?"

She exhales sharply. "Why did you bind your life to Mel's?"

Seriously? She has to ask. "She'd be dead if I hadn't."

"So?" she mutters.

I glare at her. "So, what?"

She lifts her eyebrow. "Why do you care?"

"Are you serious?"

She holds my gaze and nods. "Her soul belongs to you, Leviathan." I'm not oblivious to the sharpness in her voice when she says my name. "Correct me if I'm wrong, but she'd be more useful to you dead than alive. Right?"

*Right.* But she'd also be less fun if she was my slave. I don't mention that to Faith, though. I'm not that much of an asshole. (All right, maybe I am, but I don't feel like answering the questions that might follow.) "I owe her," I say instead and that's part of the truth. "She saved me, remember?"

Verin laughs. "You owe her because she saved you?"

"I do."

He shakes his head. "Let me get this straight. You owe her because she saved you. But your life was at risk because you saved her first, so how do you still owe her?"

"He's got a point," Faith says.

"I…" I have no clue what to say to that. Mostly, because they're right. And the truth…Well, I'm not even sure I'm ready for that.

"You?" Faith pushes.

"I—"

"Faith?" a soft but confident voice rings through the air.

All eyes turn to one of the most stunning women I've ever seen. Skin the color of caramel, hair black like the feathers of a raven and curled, eyes the color of honey and a stance that screams "Don't fuck with me or you will regret it."

208

Faith jumps up and I thank Satan I was saved by the mamba bell from further questions. "Josephine," Faith says, her voice trembling. "It's been a while."

The woman nods. "Where is your mother?"

"Here and there and"—Faith shrugs—"everywhere."

"As always."

"As always," Faith agrees.

There's a quick pause. Then, Josephine sighs. "Why are you here?" Her gaze darts to me. "With a bunch of demons nevertheless."

"I...We...I—"

Berith jumps in. "Josephine?"

Josephine turns to face my sister, recognition flaring in her gaze. "Berith? Is that you?" My sister nods. "I did not expect to see you again. So soon."

"Neither did I," Berith says and I'm dying to know how they know each other, but I keep my questions under lock and key for a more appropriate time. "But it seems like fate has brought us together once more."

Josephine cocks a brow. "Fate, huh?"

Berith shrugs. "I guess so."

"All right, how can I be of assistance?"

Berith steps aside, giving Josephine a clear view of Verin and Mel. "We have a little situation."

"A little situation?" The mamba moves toward Mel. "When the crown prince of hell"—she nods in my direction—"and a hellfire-witch are dying on my doorstep, I wouldn't refer to it as a little situation."

"You know who I am?"

Her gaze darts to me. "I felt your essence the second you stepped foot in NOLA." She draws a deep breath. "Now, I know why you're here."

I struggle to get up. "So, can you help us?"

"I—"

"Mom!" A dark voice thunders through the air. "Mom, are you—" The super tall dude stops dead in his tracks, his eyes almost popping out at the sight of us. "Shit," he barks, drawing a dagger. A dagger with a gleaming red blade. "Step away, Mom. I'll—"

"Relax," his mother says, putting her hand on his shoulder. "They're not looking for a fight."

"They're demons," he yells.

"We are," Berith says, stepping toward him.

He squints, taking my sister in. "Wait, is that..." He shakes his head. "Berith?"

"It's nice to see you, Raphael." My sister smiles at him. "You look as good as the day we last met."

The giant with the muscles of a tank grins. "Well, thank you, princess."

Berith nods. "My pleasure." She smiles. "How's everyone else?"

Raphael rolls his eyes. "That's a long story."

"Can't wait to hear it," Berith replies. And the odd thing? She means it.

*Seriously, who are these people and what have they done to my I-hate-everyone-and-anyone sister?*

I swear an oath to figure it out. After Mel has gotten the antidote. "Any chance we can postpone the reunion celebration and focus on saving her?" I point at Mel.

It's only then that Raphael catches sight of Mel. "Holy shit," he barks.

"Language," his mother—who could very well be his sister—scolds.

"Sorry," Raphael murmurs. "But she looks—"

"Like she's about to bite the dust?" I shake my head. "Yeah, no kidding."

Josephine approaches Verin and runs her hand over Mel's face. The instant her fingers connect with Mel's skin, she shudders violently. "We don't have much time left," she says. Then, she turns to me and adds, "If any at all."

I'm well aware what she's saying. The chances of survival are slim. But beating the odds is sort of my thing. "She's going to make it."

Josephine sighs. "I hope you're right." Her gaze darts to Raphael. "Tell Constantin to prepare the witch hazel antidote." Raphael nods and his mother adds, "And hurry, son."

Chapter 41

*Melissani*

Ever heard of the "cold touch of death metaphor?" Yeah, well...Whoever came up with that crap never actually touched death. Contrary to all beliefs, his touch is not cold at all. The second I took the reaper's hand I felt a wave of cozy warmth in every fiber of my being. It was so strong and comforting, it pushed the pain and the cold away, giving me a moment of blissful painless joy.

A moment that ends too soon and with an order. "Open your eyes, Melissani."

I don't know why, but I don't want to. The warming touch of the reaper had calmed my racing heart and I just wanted to hold onto the serene feeling of simply existing.

"Open them," he insists softly.

And so I do, regretting it immediately. "What the—"

We stand in the middle of Times Square. I recognize the billboards and buildings instantly. I had spent the first few years after crossing the pond in this city and hung around Times Square a lot, especially during Christmas. But something is odd about this place...The energy. It feels different. I look up. The sky is a dark shade of purple and a heartbeat later, I hear them. Screams. So many bone-chilling screams I feel like my brain is about to explode. I search for their origin and spot...

*Oh, dear goddess, what the hell happened here?*

All around us, scattered like puzzle pieces, are torn limbs. Blood covers the streets, forming puddles of crimson wherever I look.

"What...What is this?"

"The future," the reaper says.

My gaze darts to his shadowy face. "The what?"

He points ahead. "Look."

A horde of people comes at us, running at an inhuman speed, daggers in their hands. The second I spot their red eyes I realize they aren't people. They're demons. "Jesus Christ, what is happening?" I bark, instinctively jumping backward.

"You'll see," the reaper says calmly as the demons attack a group of girls hiding behind a car. They're merciless as they slam the daggers in their heads, killing them instantly.

"No!" I step forward, ready to blow the creatures into oblivion, but the reaper pulls me back.

"Your powers don't work here."

"Where is here?" I ask, dread chocking me.

"One of many futures," he explains. "Unfortunately, it became a very likely one recently."

"It's likely New York will be overrun by demons?" In which world is that likely? Not in mine, that's for sure.

"Not just New York," he says. "Come." He extends his hand. "Let me show you."

I really don't want to see whatever he's got to show me, but I feel like I don't have much of a choice.

Chapter 42

*Leviathan*

Josephine guides us into one of the condos. It has typical NOLA charm—exposed brick, custom archways and an at least 150-year-old character that breathes life into the walls. I'd be seriously interested in buying one, if I weren't dying that is.

"Take her to the bedroom," the mamba says to Verin.

My brother hates to be ordered around. Yet he doesn't say a word, just quietly does as he's told. (Maybe, I am dead already and this is...Purgatory. Yes, it must be purgatory. Or worse heaven. It could be heaven.)

"Now, what?" Verin asks, the second he lays Mel down on a comfy-looking, queen-sized bed with fluffy pillows and flowery bedsheets.

Josephine's lips part, but she doesn't get the chance to answer.

"Mom?" a voice, much like Josephine's just a bit younger and less experienced shouts.

"I'm here, baby."

A moment later, Josephine's younger twin sister—in all honesty the two look very much alike—staggers into the bedroom. "Have you seen my—" She cuts off mid-sentence, drinking the scene in. "Holy shit, what the fuck?"

Josephine rolls her eyes. "What is it with my children and foul language?"

The pretty girl ignores her mother's comment and inches closer to the bed, completely disregarding the fact she's surrounded by high-ranking demons. "Is that...Is that Melissani?"

"It is," Faith says.

The girl's gaze darts to Mel's sister. "Faith," she grumbles. "What the hell are you doing here?" There's an edge to her voice, speaking of hostility.

Faith crosses her arms. "It's nice to see you too, Bonnie."

Bonnie cocks a brow. "Can't say the same."

"Bonnie," her mother interjects. "Now isn't the time."

"Right." She sighs. Then eventually takes notice of the rest of us. "Whoa, is that..."

"The crown prince of hell?" Her mother nods. "In the flesh. And—" Bonnie's gaze darts to my sister. "Berith? Berith is that really you?"

My sister flashes her a sweet smile. "Hi, B. How have you been?"

"I—" She shakes her head. "What the hell is going on?"

"Long story," Berith says.

"No shit," the mamba replies.

"We're ready!" Raphael shouts from the living room.

"For what?" Bonnie asks.

"She's been poisoned with witch hazel," Berith explains.

Bonnies gaze darts to me. "And what happened to you? You don't look so crown princely either."

215

"He bound his life to hers," Faith explains.

Bonnie's eyes go wide. "He what?" She shakes her head. "Why?"

"Can we drop the 100-questions and fix her?" I grumble, slowly losing the battle with the scorching fire searing my insides.

Raphael marches into the bedroom carrying a steaming cauldron. "The potion is ready," he says.

"How classy." I eye the cauldron. "A bit cliche but hey…" I lift my hands. "Who am I to judge?"

The comment earns me several killer-looks from all directions, except from Josephine. She is too busy placing twelve candles in a circle around the bed. "Put the potion on the nightstand and light the candles. One for each Loa." Loas are the gods most mambas pray to. A waste of time, I'd normally say, considering the gods don't give the f-word about humanity, but since they're our last chance…Well, what is it they say? When in need, one might also pray to the gods.

Raphael just lit the last candle when someone bangs against the door. "Are you expecting someone?" Raphael asks his sister.

"Me?" She looks confused. "Why me? It's Mom's place, remember?"

He sighs, seemingly knowing more than he's eager to tell. "Go to the door, B."

She eyes him skeptically. "Why?"

Another bang.

And another.

"Open the damn door," Raphael orders.

His sister eventually caves, but not without tossing a couple of curses her brother's way.

Raphael eyes Berith. "It really is a reunion, huh?"

My sister narrows her eyes. "What are you—"

"We have to talk," a male voice barks in the living room.

"We don't have to do shit," Bonnie barks back.

"Wait." Berith eyes Raphael. "Is that who I think it is?"

"You can't just ignore me!" the guy yells.

"I can, Jesse, and I did."

"Yup." Raphael sighs. "The one and only Jesse Remington."

Berith snickers. "Well, this should be fun."

"It would be," Raphael says. "If your witch friend weren't dying in my mother's bed."

"At least one of you has his head in the game," I grumble, tired of being front and center in a telenovela of which I obviously missed the first season.

"B, please." The guy—Jesse or whatever—pleads. "Can we just talk?"

"No!"

Josephine draws a deep breath and eyes the door. "Someone should fill him in. He won't be happy to see a bunch of high-ranking demons in my bedroom and I can't have him interrupting the ritual."

"I'll go," Berith says.

But for a dying demon, I'm incredibly fast and already out of the bedroom.

## Chapter 43

*Melissani*

I blink my eyes open and face a massive sandstone colored building. Its architecture practically screams Europe. Upon closer inspection, I immediately recognize the high fountain in the center underneath the arch of said stone building—the Trevi Fountain. "Rome?" I ask the reaper. *Again?* Can't believe I'm saying this, but I wouldn't mind never stepping foot into the city again.

He nods.

"The real Rome or hell's version of it?" I double check.

"The real one," he assures me.

"O-kay." I look around. "And what are we doing in real Rome?" Don't get me wrong, I always wanted to see the eternal city and I appreciate that the reaper took me here before I bite the dust, but I don't really get the point of this little trip.

"You have to see." He looks at me. "In case, you survive."

"See what?" I ask, choosing to ignore the "in case you survive part," because I really don't want to get my hopes up.

He points ahead at the larger-than-life sized statue of the nautical god Neptune. He's being pulled to the sea on his shell-shaped chariot by two winged horses.

It's a beautiful image. The horses, one obedient and calm, the other boisterous, are a sight to behold too and if my memory serves me right, they symbolize the changing tide of the sea. The view is mesmerizing but also somehow wrong. The statue of the god is supposed to be sandstone colored not splashed with red.

"What the—" I inch closer to the water. Water that isn't blue. It's a sea of crimson, colored by the blood of the lifeless humans floating face down.

A scream pierces the night. I spin on my heels, catching sight of a girl running as if the devil himself is chasing her. "What is happening?" I ask the reaper.

He only sighs and says, "What will happen all over the world."

An instant later, a bunch of teenage boys round the corner, chasing the girl. Their eyes gleam red—demons.

"End times," the reaper says.

My gaze darts from the demons to him. "End times? As in the end of the world?"

"Yes."

"How?" I bark. "Why?"

He shoves his shadowy hands into the pocket of his long black cape. "I'll show you." He grabs my wrist and then—

Chapter 44

*Leviathan*

I reach the living room, breathing like a 100-year-old grandfather who should have long cut down on the cigarettes, or never had one in the first place. It's pathetic, really. And on any other day, I'd worry about my reputation (I'd never hear the end of it if someone saw me like this), but the instant I sense the "I'm a hero and would lay down my life for you" aura radiating off a tall, muscled guy with wavy brown hair and deep brown eyes, I find myself in the midst of a catch-22 and am torn between worrying about myself and my siblings and the witches present in this very condo. Because the guy—currently running a hand through his disheveled hair while arguing with the high-priestess's daughter—isn't just your ordinary Joe. Nope, his scent—the rotten scent of a witch-hunter—covers him and I'm wondering why the hell Raphael (he obviously knew who banged on the door) allowed his sister to open said door for a witch-hunter. Does he hate her so much that he sent her straight into the arms of death? That would be cruel, even for my standards. (And I am the cruelest of them all, if one can believe a man like Hitler.)

"Just give me a chance," the hunter pleads with Bonnie.

What? He pleads with her? Why isn't he

slaughtering her? I mean, shouldn't he prepare a green-wood pile or something? I'm confused.

Bonnie crosses her arms. "A chance to do what? Stab me in the back like you did with Manda?"

"I didn't stab Manda in the back," he barks, appearing close to losing his marbles. (Though since he is arguing with a mamba instead of killing her, he might have already lost them.)

"Oh, you didn't?" Bonnie laughs.

"I—" He cuts himself off. "She forgave me, okay? Why can't you do the same?"

She inches closer, breathing fire at him. "I'm not Manda, Jesse. And I'll never forget what you've done." She averts her gaze. "I can't. So, why don't you leave me the hell alone?"

"Because we are friends," he replies.

"Friends?" Bonnie laughs. "Friends don't lie to each other, and they sure as hell don't go sacrificing said friend's best friend to save a brother."

"That's not fair," he argues.

"Yeah, well." Bonnie shrugs. "Life never is."

The mamba has a point and usually I'd sit back and enjoy watching her break his precious hunter heart—yup, the bitter taste of love settles on my tongue and all of a sudden Raphael's reaction makes sense—but I'm not in the mood for a hunter-mamba love drama. We've got bigger fish to fry. So, I clear my throat and say, "I think it's fairly obvious the lady doesn't want you here."

The instant his gaze darts to me, the second I catch his attention, I regret it. It has little to do with his menacing frown and everything with the fact that he pulls his gun on me quicker than I can say cheese.

"What the fuck?" he barks. "That's a demon, B."

"No." She flashes him a devilish grin. "It's the crown prince of hell, actually."

"He's what?" Jesse or whatever his name is shoots daggers at me. "You're—"

"Leviathan," I say, steading myself against the brick arch. "And you are obviously a hunter with no manners."

His finger moves to the trigger of his blued Beretta, and he never takes his gaze off me, not even when he speaks to Bonnie. "Care to tell me why the crown prince of hell is lounging in your mom's living room?"

"No," she replies because obviously she's that stubborn.

"B!" he barks. "Why am I standing in front of"—he drinks me in—"an upper level demon, who looks like he's seconds from going back to hell?"

"You are so rude." (I could never look that bad. I'm stunning even when I'm dying.) "And surely, there's no need to be uncivilized."

"You're a demon," he barks.

"A handsome, powerful demon," I say.

The hunter's eyes go wide. "What madness is this, B?"

Bonnie rolls her eyes. "It's none of your business, Jesse. So, why don't you do us all a favor and hit the road." She cocks a brow. "I'm sure you've got places to be, witches to betray and girls to screw." Oh, Lord Satan, there's a lot of history between those two. Too much for a dying demon to endure.

"The crown prince of hell is standing before me," he hisses. "That sort of makes this my business or did you forget what I am?"

"How could I?" she shoots back.

The hunter sighs. "Look, B. I get you're pissed at me, and you have every right—"

"Damn right, I have every right," she cuts him off. "And FYI, I don't need your permission to be pissed at you." She throws her hands in the air. "Damn, I don't need anything from you." She steps between the hunter and me. "Now, get out."

He shakes his head. "I won't leave you with this thing."

"I'm a prince, you moron."

Bonnie laughs. "Hear that? He's a prince not a frog like you." She points to the door. "Now, get out."

"No!"

"Yes!"

"No!"

"Guys," I interfere. "Why don't we all just—"

"Shut up," they yell in unison and my temper starts to flare to life.

I'm two seconds from silencing them both forever, when my sister appears by my side. "Hello, Jesse." She flashes him a brilliant smile. "You look good."

The hunter squints, assessing my sister's vessel. It takes him a second until he recognizes her. "Berith?"

My sister shrugs. "Did you miss me?"

The hunter's gaze darts from Berith to Bonnie and eventually to me. "Someone better tell me what the hell is going on here." He holsters his gun. "Like right now!"

Bonnie refuses to comply.

Berith, however, takes a step forward, points at me and says, "Jesse, may I introduce you to my brother Leviathan."

"Your brother?" He sighs. "The crown prince of hell is your brother?"

Berith shrugs. "You know how it is, can't pick your family, can you?"

"Hey." I cast Berith a dirty look. "Was that necessary?"

She shrugs. "You secured us a spot on Hell's Most Wanted list. So, yeah, it was necessary."

"Hell's Most Wanted list?" The hunter shakes his head. "All right, what the hell did I miss?"

"Come," Berith waves him toward the bedroom. "I'll show you."

# Chapter 45

*Leviathan*

The hunter freezes at the sight of the scene unfolding in the bedroom. "Jesus," Jesse hisses as his gaze darts over the odd scenario.

Bonnie's mother sits atop Mel's lifeless body, looking up at the ceiling with eyes the color of snow. She's chanting something I can't quite make out because I'm too focused on Mel. Her veins are black like charcoal, slithering all across her face, down her neck toward her heart. The poison has spread and infiltrated her entire body. No wonder I'm barely able to walk. Verin holds Mel down, his attention fully focused on her. Which is a good thing, considering there's a hunter in the room. (My brother hates hunters. Ever since that incident with the witch he swore to kill, the one that got offed by a hunter instead.) And Faith…Well, Faith retreats to the corner of the room the second she feels the presence of said hunter. *Smart girl.*

"What the hell is going on?" the hunter whispers to Berith.

My sister keeps her gaze steady on Bonnie's mother, who now lifts something that looks like an old Athame to carve symbols in the air. "That's Melissani," she explains, pointing to Mel. "She's a hellfire witch."

"A what?" the hunter asks, quizzically. For someone who makes a living killing witches, he seems

225

to know very little about them.

Bonnie brushes past him. "She's half elemental-witch, half demon."

The hunter draws a deep breath, probably trying to calm his nerves. "Half witch, half demon, huh?"

Bonnie shrugs. "That's what I said."

"And what happened to her?" he asks Berith.

"Long story short, she went toe to toe with my father," Berith replies.

"Your father?" the hunter questions.

"The king of hell," I add.

"Wait!" He eyes the both of us. "Your father is Lucifer?"

Berith laughs. "No, Jesse. Lucifer isn't the reigning king."

"He's not?" He looks totally bewildered. "But—"

"It's complicated," Berith explains. "Remember, when I told you Lucifer was away, taking care of some family business?" He nods. "Well, he left the throne to our father. And my brother here"—she points at me—"managed to fuck up pretty badly by falling in love with"–she nods at Mel—"a witch."

"I did not fall in love," I argue, but my voice is barely a whisper and for the first time in my demonic life I'm being ignored by everyone present.

"God, that sounds totally fucked up," he says.

"Anyway," Berith goes on. "He was supposed to kill her but saved her instead. Then she saved him and now she's dying while the rest of us are on Hell's Most Wanted list."

"And here I thought my family was weird," the hunter murmurs.

"Speaking of your family, how is your brother and

his witch?"

A regretful frown hardens the hunter's face. It's gone in an instant. "Alex got out. He and Manda are in Salem raising their boy."

"Good for them," Berith says. "They deserve a little break after everything they endured."

"They do," the hunter says and means it. But I swear, there's a drop of sweet envy in his soul. One I would usually exploit. But usually I'm not dying, so I let it slide.

Bonnie's mother grabs the cauldron and forces the liquid down Mel's throat. I have a hard time watching her body jerk like she's a ragdoll and so I focus on the hunter instead. "How do the two of you know each other again?"

"Long story," the hunter says.

"I'm good with a summary," I say, not letting this one slide.

Berith sighs. "Do you remember the mission I was given by Lucifer?"

Of course, I do. It was the first time in a very long time our true king showed his face in hell. Yup, he simply walked in on us having a few shots with Marilyn (Yes, Monroe. Why do you think all male Kennedy's die so tragically young and under such weird circumstances?) and demanded to talk to my sister in private. By the time he left, Berith's face was ashen, but she refused to fill Verin and I in. Instead, she packed her stuff and was gone for months. "What about it?"

Berith points to the hunter. "He, his brother, and said brother's girlfriend were my mission. I was supposed to make sure the witch survived."

"Why would Lucifer care about a witch?" I didn't

get it. I thought he hated them like Father did.

"She's not just any witch," my sister says. "She's an untouchable and the protector of the gates to hell."

"Whoa." Did she just say an untouchable? "I thought they were extinct." At least, that's what our father has anyone believe.

"She's the last of her kind," Berith explains. "Well, was the last of her kind until her son was born."

"The witch has a son who is also untouchable?" This keeps getting weirder and weirder. Usually, gifts like that are passed down from mother to daughter. I've never heard of a male untouchable.

"He's not just untouchable," Berith explains. "He's also half hunter and…" She bites her lip. "A lot more."

Wait. I think I need a moment to swallow this. "You're saying a witch hunter fell in love with a witch and they had a witch slash hunter child?"

"Yup."

*And here I thought my life was weird.*

"Anyway," Berith says. "I told you it's a long st—"

Mel's piercing scream cuts right through Berith's sentence.

My chest constricts as my gaze darts to her. "What the—" She convulses on the bed to the point where Verin can barely hold her down. "What is happening?" In hindsight, I wonder why I bothered to ask. I felt the excruciating pain, rippling through my cells like a wildfire. It's so bad, I lose my footing and stumble against the chest of drawers. "Shit."

"Are you okay?" Berith is beside me in an instant. "Lev?"

"I'm…" I can barely breathe. "I'm good."

"What's wrong with him?" the hunter asks.

"He bound his life to hers," Berith explains and for that I get a look from the hunter that's a mixture between "Seriously?" and "Whoa, impressive."

I pay no attention to them and concentrate on Bonnie's mother. "What…is…happening?"

"The antidote," she says. "It's trying to fight the poison."

"Trying?" I ask.

"Well…" She climbs from the bed, wiping her hands on her trousers. "The infection spread to her heart." Sadness tugs at her lips. "There's no guarantee she'll make it."

"Oh, that's just—"

"Shit." The hunter draws his gun quicker than Wyatt Earp and turns to the living room.

"What is it?" Bonnie asks.

"Demons," he replies. "Can't you feel them?"

I couldn't, but Berith…Berith goes pale. "Not just any demons," she says. "Bounty hunters."

Oh, great. Because we weren't fucked enough, huh?

## Chapter 46

*Melissani*

*Hello, darkness, my old friend...* I never thought I'd say that, but I'm actually thrilled to see you again. I prefer anyplace to a Rome or New York overrun by demons. Even death's creepy waiting room is a better option than a front row seat to the world's end.

The reaper's dark eyes roam my face. Whatever it is he sees, it can't be good, because he says, "We're running out of time."

"Because I'm dying?" I ask, the pain rearing its ugly head in my chest.

He tilts his head. "That's yet to be decided, but this little journey will soon end." He meets my gaze. "One way or the other. And therefore, we must hurry."

"Hurry?" I laugh. "And here I thought death was eternal."

"Nothing lasts forever," he shoots back. "Not in this world or the next."

"Oh, so we're back to being all cryptic again, huh?" I roll my eyes. "I guess that means there's no point in asking why the hell you gave me a peep-show of the end of the world."

The reaper turns away from me. "You must understand, my dear Melissani, I am one of many, but all of us are forbidden from interfering."

"O-kay." I'm not really following. "And?"

"And there's only so much I can say without tossing the world into chaos."

"Chaos?" I sigh. "You just took me to a future where demons slaughter folks in public squares. How much more chaos could there be?"

"The possibilities are infinite," he replies, the drop of his voice raising the hairs on the back of my neck. "And therefore, we must tread carefully."

"I have no clue what you're saying," I admit, torn between ripping my own hair out and succumbing to the searing fire torturing my chest.

"Your death would be the beginning."

"Of what?"

"Of the end." He sighs.

All right, I'm sort of flattered he thinks my life is so important that my death could bring about the end of times, but that's total bullshit. "Look, not to be an asshole, but I'm just a witch. What's me pushing daisies got to do with the end of the world?"

"You have never been *just* a witch and until you accept that, the world is at great risk."

"Risk from what?" Why do I even care? I'm dying, remember?

"He will commit one act of pure sin, will betray the one he swore allegiance to and with that, the scales will be forever tipped."

"Who is he?"

Hollow black eyes meet mine. "The one you fought once, the one I'm hoping you survive to fight again."

"I fought a lot of demons and humans," I mutter. "Any chance you could be a bit more specific?"

He shakes his head. "Know this, my dear Melissani. If you live through this, if by some miracle they can save you, you must stop him at all costs."

"Okay, I'm confused." And angry. Confused and angry is never a good combination. "How am I supposed to stop someone if I don't know who? And why me? Can't you just...I don't know, kill him?" Hello, he's a reaper. He could have even killed baby Hitler. My gaze shoots to him. Why didn't he kill baby Hitler? He must have known what the dude was going to grow up to do, right?

"Evil is needed," he says. "And sometimes it takes evil to defeat evil."

"How Guru-like," I mutter. "Shame, I still don't get it."

"If you survive, you will have no choice but to accept your fate." He smiles. "It is after all the queen that wins a game of chess."

I'm all set to yell at the reaper for being so damn cryptic, when I feel a blaze of fire. "What the hell?" It starts in my toes and quickly floods my whole damn body, setting me on fire. Literally. And I'm not talking about the good kind of fire, I'm talking about the kind that killed hundreds of my sisters in the past.

"It's time," he says. "One way or the other, we will meet again." He vanishes. Leaves me alone in the dark as the flesh burns off my damn bones and all that's left for me to do is scream.

Chapter 47

*Leviathan*

When I was a younger, less experienced (still incredibly handsome) demon, I enjoyed the unique taste of chaos and mayhem (even the sweetest Baklava can't compare to it) so much, I often revisited ancient battles. Amongst my favorite were the Battle of Cannae, 216 BC, where general Hannibal outsmarted the Romans and the result was a loss of 50,000 souls, and the Battle of Gettysburg in 1863, a fight that turned the tide of the American Civil War in favor of the Union and cost over 46,000 soldiers their lives. A lot of those soldiers ended up with a one-way ticket to the pit and most of them are still there, reliving those battles day in and day out, dying over and over until the end of time. It's a bit ironic, considering they all believed they'd go to heaven because they fought for the right reasons. It's a shame none of their holy books ever mentioned that heaven and hell don't differentiate between murderers. A life taken—no matter the reason—is a life taken and only a handful of souls ever find absolution for such a crime. Anyways, the point I'm trying to make is death and destruction always excited me, and I thoroughly enjoy watching humans slaughter each other for a piece of land which in reality belongs to the goddess Gaea. So, usually I'd enjoy the chaos that's about to descend on us, but when you're the one on the battlefield and chances are you're about to lose your head—literally—your perspective shifts.

"They're close," Berith mutters, her gaze darting from me to Mel. She's still lying on the bed, convulsing, and screaming as if someone is branding her with a hot iron. And I...I'm barely able to stand, feeling her pain as if it is my own. And in a way it is.

The hunter aka Jesse doesn't waste any time. He faces the door with his drawn gun, ready to do what needs to be done. Little does he know bullets won't do him any good in this fight. "Someone better tell me who those bastards are."

"Bounty-hunters," I croak. "And I hate to break it to you, but your gun won't do you any good." (There, I said it. Warned a hunter. That's how far it's come.)

He looks over his shoulder, flashing me a wicked smile. "This isn't just a gun, dumbass."

"It looks like gun," I shoot back. "Also, your manners are truly awful."

"Yeah." He sighs, ignoring the comment about his lack of civility. "But the bullets are enchanted."

"Manda?" Berith asks with a smile.

The hunter shrugs. "She insisted."

"Smart witch," my sister says, admiration in her eyes.

I lean against the wall, trying to keep my vessel from falling apart. "Enchanted bullets or not," I hiss through gritted teeth. "We're still dead." That's harsh, I know. It's true, nevertheless. Even if Mel weren't fighting for her life and even if I were at full strength, we'd still be dead. I sense the bounty-hunters. It's a legion, and we are—my gaze darts over the faces of anyone present—not enough.

Josephine straightens her blouse. "If we die," she says. "We die fighting."

Raphael nods. "Agreed."

Constantin, who seems to be the brooding, quiet type, cracks a wicked grin and

Bonnie adds, "Besides, we've survived worse, haven't we?"

Berith laughs. "We have."

"All right." Verin rolls his shoulders back and grins. "Let's party."

I don't see how this is a party, but I do appreciate the spirit. "Aim for the head," I tell the hunter as all hell descends on us.

It starts with a deafening *bang*—the sound of the front door being blown to bits and pieces. The hunter rushes into the living room, raining bullets on my demonic brothers. Bonnie follows him, so do Raphael, Constantin, Verin and Berith. I push myself off the wall, dragging myself to the door, but Josephine blocks me. "You're in no condition to fight," she says. "Stay with her. We've got this."

I shake my head. "You have no idea what these demons are capable of."

The high-priestess laughs. "Never underestimate a mamba," she says and then she's out the door, joining the battle of New Orleans. Deep down I hope I get the chance to revisit this one, but when an invisible hand reaches for my heart, crushing it, I'm fairly certain I'll never get the chance to do anything anymore.

Gunfire echoes off the walls.

Screams erupt.

"Get down, B," the hunter yells.

"Behind you," Berith barks.

"There are too many," Verin admits.

And me? I'm on my knees, forcing air into my lungs. Or at least, I'm trying. And I'm failing. Because all of a sudden, the noises—battle cries of the demons and my unlikely defenders alike—cease and all I see is…

Darkness.

# Chapter 48

*Leviathan*

Utter and complete darkness wraps around me. I blink again and again, but my eyes refuse to adjust. (Yes, yes, you think demons have night vision, don't you? Newsflash: We don't.) Despite my lack of sight, I'm well aware of the shift in the atmosphere. I'm no longer in Josephine's bedroom. Frankly, I'm not sure if I'm even still alive.

"Hello?" a faint whisper arouses my attention, the voice familiar and close.

"Mel?" I turn around, searching this devilforsaken place for her. "Mel, is that you?"

"L-Lev?" she stammers. "Where are you?"

"I'm here," I say.

"Here is a super vague term," she grumbles and despite everything, I realize she hasn't lost her snark.

"Keep talking," I say. "I'll find you."

"Keep talking?" She laughs. "What do you want me to say? Nice to see you? What brings you to death's waiting room?"

"Death's waiting room?" Is that where we are? It makes sense. I've heard stories of this place and every soul—bound for hell—who's ever been here spoke of impenetrable darkness. The kind I'm currently facing.

"What are you even doing here?" Mel asks.

I move slowly, following her voice. "Dying, I

suppose."

"What?" she barks. "Why?"

I draw a sharp breath. "Long story."

"I've got nothing but time," she replies.

I bump against a wall or something and swallow the curse sitting on the tip of my tongue. "Well," I say, ignoring the sharp pain in my shoulder. "Let's just say, I was a bit reckless."

"Reckless with your life?" Her tone suggests she doesn't believe a word I'm saying. "That doesn't sound like you."

"Yeah, well…" It doesn't. Or didn't. But… "Demons can change, you know."

"Bullshit," she hisses, her voice much closer than before. "Tell me what happened. Faith…Oh god, is she okay? Is she—"

"She was fine," I say.

"Was?"

"Well, I'm currently dying, so I can't really tell you what's happening in the other world, can I?"

She sighs. "I suppose not."

Heat billows through the air. She's close. So close, I just need to extend my hand and all of a sudden, I feel her warm skin. "Got you." I pull her close, instinctively wrapping my arms around her. "I've got you."

She snakes her arms around me, hugging me like she's never hugged me before. "I wish I could say I'm happy to see you, but…" She trails off and I understand what she's saying, even without her giving voice to it.

"I guess it could be worse, huh?"

She rests her cheek against my chest, sobbing quietly. "It is worse."

"What do you mean?"

"The reaper," she says. "He showed me the future."

Wait, what did she just say? "A reaper showed you the future?" That's impossible. Reapers are neutral, they can never interfere and they sure as hell don't show dying witches glimpses of the future.

"Not just any future," she says, her tears soaking through my shirt. "He showed me the end."

I step back. "Impossible."

"It's true," she says.

I shake my head. "Reapers are forbidden from interfering. Look"—I inch closer, rubbing my hands down her arms—"you've been through a lot. And this sort of darkness…It can mess with the best of us."

"I didn't hallucinate," she barks.

"I didn't say you did," I reply, softly. "But maybe, you—" Lost your marbles? Are crazy? I can hardly say that, can I?

"You don't believe me?"

"I…" I wrap my arms around her and sigh. "It doesn't matter, Mel. We are going to die, so let's not waste our last minutes arguing about the end of the world, okay?"

Her muscles loosen. "I guess it would be pointless, huh?"

"Very."

Despite the darkness, I feel her eyes on me. "You won't tell me why you're dying, will you?"

"Nope."

She draws in air. "I'm sorry."

"For what?" I ask confused.

I feel her shrug. "I don't know. I just have this weird feeling you wouldn't be here if it wasn't for me. It's stupid, but—"

"I'm not sorry," I cut her off with a truth that shatters me and puts me back together at the same time.

"You're dying," she says as if that changes anything.

"Everyone has to die someday," I shoot back. "But not everyone gets to die with a hot witch in his arms. Also…" I pause. "It's not my first rodeo with death." Yeah, sure, the last time my life ended I was still human, but…Death is death. The only difference? Human me went to hell. Demon me will go to purgatory.

"Jesus." She shudders. "You almost sound human."

"Ah, come on, Mel. You're in the arms of a mesmerizing demon and fate allowed you to die in those strong arms, so don't mess it up now."

"Almost," she grumbles. "Almost."

I rest my chin on top of her head and look into the blackness. "I guess that's it then, huh?"

"Not quite," a dark husky voice says. A voice I recognize immediately.

"Sam?" I spin, searching the darkness for the reaper. "Is that you?"

"Hello, Leviathan," he confirms my suspicions. "It hasn't been long enough."

"Agreed," I hiss, age old anger flooding my system. "What are you doing here? Couldn't your boss send a more competent employee?"

He laughs. "He could have, but I volunteered."

"Because you missed me," I shoot back, balling my fists.

"Because I hoped this might happen."

"What are you—"

Mel screams like a Siren, dropping to her knees.

"Mel, what's—"

Then I feel it, too. Pain. It's like an octopus, invading my body with its tentacles, ripping my insides to shreds. I can't breathe, can't stay on my feet. And when I drop to the floor beside Mel, grabbing her hand, I feel an unnatural pull. Like a magnet. "What the—"

"Find the witch who cheated death not once, but twice," Sam yells, his voice growing more and more distant. "She will know."

Those are the last words I hear before—

## Chapter 49

*Leviathan*

The next time I open my eyes, I'm blinded by light. Not the kind that holds the promise of Nirvana and the end of suffering. Nope, just plain, old candlelight. "What the hell?" I dig my palms into the floor, pushing myself up on my knees and look around. "This isn't purgatory," I say.

"It's not," Mel agrees.

Hearing her voice forces me to my feet and even though I'm still weak, I'm no longer in pain. Just tired. Really tired. But that doesn't matter because Mel is sitting on Josephine's bed, alive and well, I should add. As well as one can be after fighting the king of hell and being covered in cuts and bruises. "Mel?" I say, afraid I might be hallucinating. Or worse ended up in a time-loop where I'm forced to lose Mel over and over until the end of days. One of the more gruesome punishments in purgatory. "Are you...Are you okay?"

She looks around, taking in the cauldron and the twelve candles. "Where are we?"

"New Orleans," I reply, approaching her slowly.

She narrows her eyes. "New Orleans? Why?"

"Because your sister told us Josephine was the only one with an antidote for the witch-hazel."

"Josephine Lacroix?" Mel's eyes are saucepan wide. "Bonnie's mother?"

"That's the one."

"And she agreed to help?" She sounds truly surprised, and I make a mental note to ask her about the beef Josephine and her mother have.

"Without hesitation," I admit.

"Whoa." She eyes me. "That's...Weird."

I sigh. "I'm just glad it worked." I really didn't feel like dying today.

Mel looks around. "And where is everyone?"

"Oh, no." I didn't even realize the gunfire had ceased, that no one is screaming and it's too damn quiet.

Mel is on her feet in a heartbeat. "What is going on?"

"I almost forgot."

"Forgot what?" she barks, being her old bitchy self again.

"Bounty-hunters," I say. "They stormed the place. Moments before I..."

"Faith." Mel is paler than a ghost. "Where is Faith?"

"I don't know," I answer honestly.

Mel is out the door in a heartbeat.

## Chapter 50

*Melissani*

Someone once told me everyone's story is merely a retold fairy tale. It's the reason why most girls are hunting their happily-ever-after with dreamy prince charming. But if that someone is right, if everyone's story truly is a retold fairytale, mine would be classified as the untraditional kind, the Brothers Grimm kind of stuff. You know, the sort that too often ends in death, gore, and chaos.

Death: the cozy living room is littered with bodies. The stink of rotten eggs and sulfur says the newly deceased spent their last minutes being possessed by demons.

Gore: blood covers the walls, the furniture, the floor. It's an ocean of crimson and the sight brings forth memories of the Trivi Fountain.

Chaos: my sister screams. The sound pierces my heart and forces my feet to run out the door, down a flight of stairs, right into a back alley crawling with demons.

"Shit," Lev barks beside me. No clue how he got here so quickly, but he's obviously less affected by almost dying than I am. Seriously, I'm breathing like a grandmother and my knees shake like hell. "This doesn't look good."

"You think?" I hiss through gritted teeth, scanning

the horde of demons, surrounding my sister, Lev's siblings, the Lacroixs and a dude I've never seen before, one whose vibes scream, "Run, Melissani. Run!"

Lev ignores my sharp comment and straightens his shoulders. "Looks like we're going to have some fun, huh?"

"You and I"— I say, picking up a scythe that once belonged to a demon—"have a very different idea of fun."

"Oh, come on," he says, grinning like the cocky demon bastard he is while pulling out his dagger. "It's just like old times." Of course, I know what the prick is referring to. I just don't do him the favor of acknowledging how right he is. Instead, I straighten my back, draw a deep breath, and focus on the weight of the scythe in my hands. Silvery moonlight slithers along the white blade, a blade made of the bones of a saint—the only thing besides the bones of upper-level demons and hellfire that can kill a demon. It's a handy weapon and I don't think twice before rushing the horde of demons, running the blade straight through one of their necks. The blood of the demon's vessel—a woman in her early forties with blondish hair and blue eyes—splatters across the building wall, while her head rolls toward Lev's combat boots. Her mouth is agape, her eyes wide open and already glazing over. The vessel is dead, but so is the bounty-hunter demon who took the poor woman on her last ride. It's what the bones of a saint does to demons. They don't just send those bitches back to the pit, they obliterate them forever. That's why bounty-hunter demons carry them—to slaughter their own kind for prestige and fortune. Whatever that means in hell.

One demon down. At least twenty still circling my sister and the others. On any other day, I'd simply blow them all to hell, but after the encounter with Lev's father and being poisoned I'm running low on energy and Lev looks equally messed up. Yup, that's my kind of fairytale. The sort that picks up after a near death experience in a dark alley, behind a run-down Chinese restaurant, with a demon attack. Scratch that. These creatures aren't just ordinary, red-eyed bitches. They're skilled warriors who won't stop until we're all dead. It's ironic. I'd never given much thought to how I'd die. I used to believe the concept of death was simple enough—take your last breath and be gone. Like switching off your favorite TV-show in the middle of a fantastic scene. So damn frustrating. But if I have learned one thing in the past few hours, it's nothing about death is easy. You cannot control life and you sure as hell cannot control death. I mean, look at me. Just the other night I thought I had it all figured out. I had a plan. Conjure the crown prince of hell, who happened to be my ex. Torture the crown prince of hell, until he caved and freed my sister from her hellish prison. And last but not least, kill the crown prince of hell and rid the world of his evil once and for all. In theory, it was the perfect plan. In reality? Not so much. Like any Brothers Grimm story, it started to go downhill when I put my trust in a treacherous witch, who betrayed me, and it reached its peak, when I saved the damn crown prince of hell by battling his father, the king of hell, instead of killing him. On the bright side, I've got my sister back. On the not so bright side, we— that would be said crown prince, his two siblings,

Berith and Verin, my sister, Faith, and I—are now officially on Hell's Most Wanted list and the king has sent his best warriors after us. Warriors who won't rest until we're all dead. I guess happy endings aren't for hellfire witches like me, huh?

"There are too many of them," Faith screams. Her voice is thick. I can practically taste her dread.

"Fall back," Verin orders like he's some kind of major in our army of misfits.

The dude with the gun frowns, taking aim and shooting some of the demons between the eyes. They die on impact. I'd ask Lev how bullets can kill demons, but I'm a little busy severing the heads of said demons' vessels.

One by one they go down, but my sister wasn't wrong. There are just too many of them and they draw closer to our friends, or enemies—the jury is still out on that one.

Josephine Lacroix steps forward, lifting her palms. "It won't hold them for long," she barks at the others, as she throws her head back and chants a protection spell.

Her son—I believe his name is Constantin—moves forward, whispering words that send the essence of one of the demons, the closest one, back to hell.

Bonnie—Josephine's daughter and my sister's frenemie—grabs her mother's hand, using her magic to strengthen her mother's protective shield.

Verin, Berith and Faith join the battle, slicing throats and pulling out hearts.

But every time one of the bitches goes down, another rounds the corner to take its place.

"Fall back," Verin repeats as more demons join the

fight.

"Fall back where?" Gun Guy yells. "We're practically sitting ducks." He has a point. This is a one-way street, and I don't see how any of us will make it out in one piece.

"Lev!" I shout. "We have to do something."

He holds a heart in his hand and rolls his eyes. "What does it look like I'm doing?"

I'd rather not answer that question. Like ever. "They'll overrun us," I bark instead.

"No," Lev says. "They won't."

Berith and Verin push toward us, killing demon after demon.

So, does Gun Guy. He shoots them with one hand, stabs them with the other. Impressive.

I run the scythe through another neck, listening to the sound of a head plopping to the ground. "We're going to die in the back alley of a damn Chinese restaurant."

"We won't." Lev sounds so certain I almost believe him. "It's going to be okay,"

"O-kay?" Berith laughs. "I don't think this"—she points ahead at the demons rounding the corner— "classifies as okay."

He smiles that half-smile. The one that exposes him as the ruthless demon crown prince he truly is. "Cheer up, sis. Between the five of us, the voodoo brigade and the witch hunter they don't stand a chance."

Verin shakes his head. "Your pride is going to be the end of us."

"Drama queen," Lev shoots back as the demons draw closer.

Wait. "Did you say witch hunter?"

Lev eyes the gun dude. "Right, you haven't been introduced." He grabs a demon by the neck and snaps it. "Mel," he says. "Meet Jesse." He nods at the hunter. "Jesse, meet Mel."

The hunter nods back, then puts a bullet through another brain.

My sister has obviously had enough of all this shit. "Why don't you use your darkness to get us all out of here alive?"

"Because he can't," I say.

"Why?" my sister asks.

Same reason I can't use my hellfire. "He's too weak." The showdown with his father and almost dying took a toll on both of us and I fear we might not have enough juice left to send these assholes back to hell.

Lev's gaze darts to me. "I'm not weak."

"You're not?" I laugh and gesture at the demons. "All right, then be my guest. Prove me wrong."

"I...I..."

"Enough bickering," Berith yells. "We need a plan."

"I have a plan," Lev shoots back.

"Which is?" Verin asks.

Lev shrugs. "Fight."

"A legion of bounty-hunters?" Berith shakes her head. "We're so going to die."

"Less drama," Lev barks. "More fighting."

Seriously, why the fuck I continuously listen to the prick remains a mystery to me. Shouldn't I know better? Shouldn't I be smarter? Shouldn't I...I don't know, maybe burn his princely ass myself before I'm ever tempted to put my trust in him again? Let's be real for a second. I knew we were beyond fucked when Lev disobeyed his father's orders to kill me. You don't mess with the king of hell and get away with it. Nope, you get a damn death sentence for it. And this…This is us walking the green mile. A mile paved with demonic bounty-hunters coming at us. Hard.

"Watch out!" I shout as the horde launches another attack. Twenty demons, carrying swords and scythes made from the bones of saints, rush us at once.

Berith closes her eyes. A moment later, thick black smoke crawls along the paved street and wraps around the vessels of two demons, snapping their necks and sending them back to the pit.

Verin seems to prefer a good old fist fight. One second, he's next to us. The next, he's somewhere between the bounty-hunters, cracking bones and scattering teeth across the cement.

Despite her trembling hands, my sister holds her own. She uses her powers to bring down a bunch of flowerpots hanging on someone's balcony up above. They crack the heads of two demons.

The Lacroixs keep up the chanting, expanding the protective shield to all of us. Constantin on the other hand uses his magic to send the demons back to the pit.

The hunter—who I should fear even more than those demons—puts demon after demon down, shooting them like rabid dogs.

Lev too joins the fight. But just like I suspected he doesn't use his power. He uses his fists like Verin.

And I? Well, I have a scythe and I use it to sever more heads. Heads of vessels. Heads of humans, who were unlucky enough to be targeted by demonic bounty-hunters.

We fight. We kill. We manage to stay alive. But the bounty-hunters are like the damn Hydra. Every time we take one down, two more show up. "We've got to get the hell out of here," I scream.

"How?" Berith asks.

I look around, searching for an escape route. There's none. "No clue, but—"

"Mel," Lev's sharp cry echoes off the walls of the building, a brick wall structure that must have lasted several generations. "Get down! Get down now!"

I hear him. And no, I don't ignore the prick deliberately. Though, he surely deserves my ignorance. The problem is my body is in no shape to duck as quickly as needed. Lev's father did a real number on me. I'm talking bruised (maybe even broken) ribs, a swollen eye, and a split lip to mention a few. So, I simply stand there and glare at the scythe that's about to come down on me.

"For fuck's sake, Mel! Move!" Lev pushes me out of harm's way seconds before the blade can take my head. I land in a puddle of what smells like human pee. The stuff soaks through my jeans and reminds me how badly I need to shower. "Are you okay?" he asks, offering me his hand.

I ogle his outstretched hand and I know I should take it, should get up and fight. The whole alley is crawling with bounty-hunters. They've caged us in and everyone—even my little sister Faith—is engaged in battle, a battle we're losing.

"Get up," Lev says softly. "You have to get up."

What I have to do is end this madness once and for all. I should bring out the fire that burns within my soul, turning those stupid fuckers to ash and dust. I should do what I do best—kill demons. Instead, I sit on the damn ground, watching the demon, who tried to have my head, approach. "Lev," I manage to say, pointing at the demon.

Lev turns, smiling smugly. "Oh, hey!" He looks the bounty-hunter up and down. "Nice meat-suit."

Silvery hair, hawk-shaped nose, big blue eyes, and a plaid shirt stained with what appears to be ice-cream—fifty bucks says the bounty-hunter snatched this vessel in the park while the poor dude, whose soul once occupied this body, took his grandkids for ice-cream. "My prince," the demon says, bowing low and grinning like the cat that ate all the canaries and got away with it. "I have no quarrel with you and it's nothing personal, but my orders are clear. So, why don't you do us all a favor and come back to hell with us? Your father wants to talk to you."

Talk? I laugh. "Yeah, right."

"Hm." Lev taps his forefinger against his temple. "Let me think about it." He tests the thing's patience, stretching the moment eternally. Then, he replies cheerfully. "Nope, not interested."

Grandpa-demon sighs. "Then, you leave me with no choice, my prince."

Lev's wholehearted laughter vibrates through my body. "You really believe you stand a chance, don't you?"

"I am Buer," Grandpa-demon roars like a lion. "Commander of fifty legions and—"

"And I'm bored." He smiles an angelic smile. "Demons." He shrugs. "So full of themselves." A heartbeat later, he snaps his fingers and Grandpa-demon quite literally turns to stone.

I'd be seriously impressed with his Medusa-skills, if there weren't at least ten other demons coming at us with drawn saint-bone-swords. Lev pulls me to my feet, grinning like we aren't about to be demon food. "This was fun," he says, his gaze darting to Berith. She's surrounded by a horde of hipster-demons. Verin is next to her snapping neck after neck, but whenever one goes down, another shows up out of nowhere. And Faith...She's just a few steps away, scratching some biker-demon's eyes out, while Gun Dude reloads and the Lacroixs fight to keep the protection spell in place. "However"—Lev's eyes find mine—"We should cut this short and get the hell out of here."

"Great idea." I snort. Question is how are we going to escape if the bounty-hunters keep multiplying?

"So, what do you think?" he asks, snapping his fingers again and turning another demon to stone. "Can you roast the idiots?"

I don't know. I can feel the fire roaring inside me. However, my gifts are off balance. To be honest, I'm a little worried I might burn my sister, his siblings, the Lacroixs or that handsome witch hunter instead of the demons.

"Mel," the urgency in Lev's voice tugs at my heart. He's worried. I sense the bitter stink of it. "You need to—"

"I know what I need to do." I close my eyes, draw a deep breath, and follow the heat within me. It takes me to the depths of my soul, where sparks of hellfire dance to an unsteady rhythm.

"No pressure," Lev mutters. "But anytime now would be great."

"No pressure, huh?" *Idiot.*

"Impact in three, two—"

"Shut up," I bark as I focus on one of the sparks, allowing it to grow into a fully fleshed flame. Once it's big enough, I open my eyes again and spot at least forty more demons about to overrun us. "Shit!"

"Do something," Lev orders.

And for once, I don't argue. Instead, I let the flames consume me and when I feel the surge of power pushing through the palms of my hands, I toss the greenish flames at the bounty-hunters.

They scream in agony as the flames devour them whole, wiping their essences off the face of the earth.

"Well done." Lev applauds me. "But you forgot some." His gaze darts to the left, where our siblings and new friends are fighting for their lives.

I offer Lev the sweetest and most murderous glance and sigh. "You could help."

"I could," he admits. "But watching you is more fun. And hotter." He nods to himself. "Definitely hotter."

I can't believe him. "Jesus Christ—"

"Is dead," Lev cuts in. "And they"—he points to the demons—"should be, too."

Arguing with a prick like him is pointless, so I close my eyes, find another spark in the pit of my soul and toss the ball of hellfire at the demons.

They scream like a bunch of little girls as death claims their souls.

Chapter 51

*Leviathan*

"You're staring," Mel grumbles as exhaustion washes over her face and she steadies herself against the dumpster of the Chinese restaurant.

I am. Staring, I mean. "Sorry, love, I can't help it." She looks like she's been through hell. And she literally has but damn me. She's sex on fire. The cut on her lip, her ripped shirt, her bruised skin, the wild red hair—it's a sight to behold. Yet, what really gets me—my gaze darts over the ashes of the bounty-hunters—is what she's capable of even when she's running on reserve.

Judging by the look on the hunter's face, I'm not the only one amazed by her performance. "Holy shit, that was…"

"Impressive?" Bonnie finishes for him and although she sounds genuine, I'm not oblivious to the sweet, sweet taste of jealousy gliding over the tip of my tongue. No matter what the mamba says, she cares about the hunter. Odd bunch of folks they are.

"I was going to go with scary," the hunter says. "But, yeah, impressive, too."

Mel leans against the cold metal, drawing deep breaths. I have a feeling she couldn't care less about the praise. "We should get out of this alley," she finally mutters.

"We should," Raphael says.

His mom and brother nod. Even my siblings and Faith agree. Wow, this has to be some kind of alternate reality. One where we aren't all arch enemies, born to slaughter each other. As I said, odd.

"He will send more," Berith whispers. "It's just a matter of time, until—"

Without a warning my sister falls silent. Her eyes are wide, her mouth open.

I step toward her. "Berith what—"

"Not a step closer," a metallic voice whispers.

I blink several times. Yet I don't see anyone. Our allies move into fighting stance, but none seem to see the assailant. Except Berith. She looks over her shoulder. Her expression frozen. "Stay where you are." At first, I think my sister speaks to whoever she sees, but when I inch closer, she barks. "Lev, don't!"

Mel is on high alert. "Berith, what's going on?"

"Can't you see her?"

"Who?" the hunter asks, scanning the area just like the rest of the group.

Berith grows paler by the second. "She's right there." She points ahead at—

"There's nothing."

"Nothing you see," the metallic voice whispers as a shadowy figure blinks into existence.

"What the fuck?" The hunter aims his gun at the…I'm frankly not sure what that is. "Is that…A demon ninja-assassin?"

For a lack of a better description. "It sure looks like it," I admit.

She laughs. The sound—like fingernails on a chalkboard—rattles my bones. "I'm honored. For I am as deadly as the best ninja-warrior."

"She doesn't have confidence issues," Bonnie remarks.

"I don't," she says. "And while I appreciate the small talk, it's time to go home." Her gaze darts from Berith to Verin to me and eventually lands on Mel.

Mel straightens and I spot the fire in her eyes. It's weak, but she's ready to use her last ounce of strength on the woman.

"I wouldn't do that," ninja-assassin says, lifting her palm. Faint moonlight reflects on the blade in her hand—a blade made of the bones of a saint. "Unless you want to get her killed." She points the tip of the blade against Berith's chest.

"Stop," I order.

"I don't serve you, Crown Prince. And I will use this on your sister quicker than your witch can use her powers." Her eyes are green like Mel's, but the rest of her face is covered. So, I can't even tell if we've had the pleasure before.

"Enough," the hunter roars as the initial shock slowly subsides. "You might be able to kill her, but you can't take all of us." He nods at Mel. "I promise you you're fried before you even try."

She bends her head to the side and chuckles. "You are right, Jesse."

"How do you know my name?" he barks.

"I know a lot," she replies. "And because I appreciate the effort all of you have put into the survival of our dear Leviathan, I'm inclined to offer you a deal."

"We don't make deals with the likes of you," Josephine says.

"Wrong." She pushes the blade a bit harder against

my sister's chest and I taste Berith's fear. It should be sweeter than honey, but somehow it tastes foul and wrong. "You haven't made such deals *yet*." Her gaze lands on Bonnie. "But never say never."

Jesse steps forward. "What's that supposed to mean?"

"Time will tell, my dear Jesse." She straightens her shoulders. "Anyway, back to my offer." She snakes her arm around Berith's hips, drawing her close. "I will give you three days to return to hell," she says to me. "Bring your witch with you and your sister and your bunch of"—she eyes the group—"heathens will live. Disobey me," she warns, her eyes flaring like a green flame. "And all of you will die."

I'm all set to send the nasty bitch to hell myself, but the second I take a step, she dematerializes with my sister in tow.

"What the fuck was that?" the hunter asks.

"I have no clue," I admit.

"She's got Berith," Verin barks, close to pulling his hair out. "We've got to do something."

"Yeah," I say. "No kidding."

"What, though?" Raphael eyes the spot where seconds ago the ninja-assassin stood. "She's—"

"Powerful," his mother finishes for him. "Very, very powerful."

"We have to find the witch that cheated death not once but twice," Mel says out of the blue, looking as if she's just seen several ghosts.

"What?" I say, a bit worried about her mental health.

"That's what the reaper said, right?" She looks at me for confirmation and Sam's words come back to me.

"Yeah, I think that's what he said." I shake my head. "But how are we supposed to find said witch? We don't even know who she is."

"We do," Jesse and Bonnie say at the same time.

"Care to elaborate?"

The hunter and the witch look at each other, silent understanding in their eyes. They nod, and then Bonnie says, "There's only one witch who has cheated death not once but twice."

"Who?" my brother barks. "Who is that?"

"The same witch your sister helped to save," Jesse says.

"Amanda Bishop," Bonnie says.

Mel nods. "That's got to be her." She faces me. "We have to find her."

"And what good will that do?" I shake my head. "We don't even know why we should seek her out and Berith—"

The hunter pats my shoulder. "We'll get her back."

"We?" I almost laugh. "You're a hunter."

"And she's a friend." He eyes Bonnie. "I won't turn my back on a friend again. Not now. Not ever."

"Now he grows a conscience," Bonnie murmurs.

Mel ignores them. "What are you waiting for?" She moves out of the alley. "Let's go!"

"Why can't I shake the feeling that this is a really bad idea?"

Verin stands beside me. "Because it probably is." He sighs. "But what choice do we have?"

I could walk into my father's trap, hoping the ninja-assassin keeps her word, and lets everyone else live. The problem? My gaze lands on Mel's back. Well, the problem is I'm too damn selfish. "Let's go find the witch, then." We've got three days and the clock is already ticking.

## A word about the author…

A passionate reader and writer, addicted to the dark side of the craft. Nadine grew up with Marvel heroes and horror films. She loves stories that challenge gender stereotypes, religious beliefs and tackle topics such as racism and cultural differences in an entertaining way. Nadine has a BA in Comparative Religions and studied Creative Writing at the University of Oxford. If she isn't traveling the world, she's reading, writing, or watching movies.

Thank you for purchasing
this publication of The Wild Rose Press, Inc.

For questions or more information
contact us at
info@thewildrosepress.com.

The Wild Rose Press, Inc.
www.thewildrosepress.com